The Marginal Ride Anthology

The Marginal Ride Anthology

Short Fiction

by

Sang Kim
Jerry Levy
Michael Mirolla
Timothy Niedermann
Ursula Pflug
Ian Thomas Shaw
Geza Tatrallyay
Caroline Vu

The Marginal Ride is a collection of short fiction.

Copyright © Ian Thomas Shaw (rights for anthology)

ISBN 978-1928049548

Published in Canada by Deux Voiliers Publishing, Aylmer, Quebec.

www.deuxvoilierspublishing.com

Anthology Editor Ian Thomas Shaw

Associate Editor Timothy Niedermann

Cover Design Ian Thomas Shaw

TABLE OF CONTENTS

The Dreams of Trees by Ursula Pflug	1
Billy by Michael Mirolla	10
Spoiled Rice by Sang Kim	17
Mai's Story by Caroline Vu	24
The Scent of Lemons by Ian Thomas Shaw	29
The Long Walk by Timothy Niedermann	37
The Writing Life by Jerry Levy	46
The Veteran and the Passerby by Geza Tatrallyay	51
The Man Who Dreamed of Being Noah by Jerry Levy	61
Lycanthropy by Michael Mirolla	76
The Phone Number by Geza Tatrallyay	84
On Fire Bridge by Ursula Pflug	96
Patsy Cline Sings Songs of Love by Sang Kim	103
The Wedding by Timothy Niedermann	110
Please, Dr. Luu by Caroline Vu	118
Ashes and Clay by Ian Thomas Shaw	123
Contributors' Bios	131

INTRODUCTION

WE ALL NEED TO BELONG—to a family, to a business, to a nation, to a cause. That sense of belonging anchors us. It helps give meaning to our lives. It makes us feel secure.

So, what does it mean to lose that, to be marginalized? One moment you feel a part of something, you are a beloved child or parent, you are a valued employee, a proud resident of a community, a loyal citizen of a nation. The next, you find yourself removed, maybe outside looking in, maybe far away in time, space, distance, or any of the other ways our bonds with each other can be broken.

How does one become marginalized? For some it is a choice, a need to pursue a different course—a passion, an obsession. Isolating, but perhaps rewarding. For others, however, marginalization is anything but that. Their lives hit a bump, an obstacle, a challenge, and suddenly all of their familiar reference points are gone. They become unmoored, drifting, lost, desperate. Often subjected to neglect and abuse, they are ready victims for the worst that society can inflict.

Eight Canadian and American writers have each contributed two stories to *The Marginal Ride* anthology. Their characters and themes are as diverse as the circumstances of marginalization itself. Ursula Pflug deals both with the pain of losing one's memory and the pain memory can bring. Michael Mirolla enters the mind of a crippled criminal and then jumps to a ritual for the victim of a werewolf. Sang Kim, who was born in Korea, describes how immigrant children watch their family life disintegrate through the lens of spoiled rice, and then weaves the Korean language into the trauma of a man losing his ability to speak. Caroline Vu, a physician who is originally from Vietnam, writes of a refugee girl losing her mother and of the relationship between a doctor and a patient with a troubled child. Ian Thomas Shaw spent years in East Africa, and he brings that experience to bear in a story about a young immigrant woman from

Eritrea now living in Italy trying to retain something of her past. He then switches gears to show how an old man remembers his life as he recedes into death. Timothy Niedermann tells of the experience of being fired from a long-time job, then takes us to Palestine for a traditional wedding, based on a true and sad event there. Jerry Levy details the loneliness of being a writer before describing the passions that drive a man who thinks he is Noah. Lastly, Geza Tatrallay relates a conversation between a pedestrian and a homeless veteran and then uses his thriller-writer skills to animate the desperate plight of trafficked women.

The characters in these stories are vastly different, of course, but what connects them is that they are all in some way removed from the secure existence that society is supposed to provide. Some want to get back to a normal life, others don't. Still others can't. We hope these stories will move you in ways you haven't experienced so that you too can gain a broader and deeper understanding of and empathy for fellow human beings who find themselves on the margins.

The Editors

THE DREAMS OF TREES

Ursula Pflug

THERE WERE SEVERAL PAIRS OF knee-high green rubber boots on the mat, including a pair that belonged to Sandrine and three that were Randy's. They were the kind of boots people wore to go fishing or hunting, with a felt lining. It wasn't possible to buy them in the city at all. She took her own shoes off by the door as she always did. Because of this almost universal rural habit, Sandrine thought, country houses generally had clean floors even when inhabited almost entirely by men.

Changing from boots into slippers, Sandrine remembered with some dismay that her husband's name wasn't Randy at all; it was Mike. Said husband was sitting at the table working on the crossword puzzle. He looked up and measured her with a lingering elevator glance from head to toe and toe to head. He didn't say a word but gave her the slightest of nods, after which he got up and put on the kettle for tea. When it was done they sat at the table and drank it.

Watching him work on his crossword she knew with a dead

certainty he wasn't called Mike—not Mike nor Randy, either. She wished he would speak and give away his name. How could she forget such a thing? It wasn't as if she were eighty-two and had dementia. She was a young woman, thirty-four, in possession of a nice house in a small Ontario town and two beautiful small children who were away for the weekend, visiting their paternal grandmother two towns over.

She also had an unusually attractive husband whose name she'd forgotten. How could that be? She knew he'd been grating on her nerves lately, to the point where she'd been indulging in escape fantasies. Was forgetting his name some kind of karmic retribution for her unkind thoughts? Sandrine did a quick mental check: had she been in a car accident or recently suffered some other serious bump to her head? Was her amnesia caused by a concussion? Alas, none of these seemed true. She simply didn't know.

Just as strangely and suddenly as her husband's name had fled, Sandrine saw in her mind's eye diagonals of green lozenges printed onto the back of the upholstery of the seat in front of her. It was a childhood memory. She'd been on the train with her father in North Africa. She didn't think of the trip often and wondered why the memory was chasing her now, taking over, hanging on, not giving up. Looking out the window at the purple-black watchman hollyhocks guarding the vegetable beds, Sandrine wondered whether she would ever remember the trip again. Memory was a strange and fickle thing. She should make a note before the image fled, perhaps on the back of the phone bill that sat on the kitchen table, with its varnished veneer top and white lacquered legs.

Sandrine looked at her husband and smiled; he was so gorgeous it was hard not to. He smiled back and bent over his crossword as if he welcomed the silence. That's what being married for a long time got you: the possibility of making and drinking tea all without needing to speak. Sandrine figured it for a good thing, most days.

She remembered camels she'd seen, slurping out of buckets at an oasis near Djerba. At some point, her father had gotten off to go on an important visit alone, and the train had sped on through the night without him. Sandrine remembered sitting alone in her seat, trying to converse with strangers in languages she didn't know well, wishing for blankets, more money, apples, friends, all of the above. In the end, she'd fallen asleep counting lozenges, noticing their patterns, how they repeated. She'd written in her journal, but not about pomegranates or camels or the magical train ride itself. Instead, she'd described the strange upholstery on the back of the seat in front of her. Sandrine had been so young at the time, a child really, thirteen or so, scribbling in a notebook that might still be in a carton in the attic. If she saw it, would she even recognize the book? Why was she thinking of it now?

She'd learned that often enough the timing and content of certain thoughts had significance. Djerba, the Island of Dreams, was in Tunisia, a country she had visited at thirteen with her father. He had wanted her to see the place of her birth and after her mother had died had used part of the insurance money to pay for the trip. Had their train really crossed the old Roman causeway to Djerba, or had they taken a bus or taxi for this last leg of the journey? It was all so long ago she wasn't sure. Maybe the train had been a dream train, just as Djerba had been Ulysses's Isle of the Lotus Eaters.

How could Sandrine even know such obscure literary trivia? Maybe, sitting on the train, she'd read a tourist brochure whose useless facts were now emerging from her subconscious like flotsam escaped from lengthy entrapment beneath the waves. Maybe some kind of mischievous metaphysical imp had taken up residence in her brain, excising important data, such as her husband's name, and replacing them with dreamy poetic childhood memories whose relevance, if any, she couldn't fathom. At least not now, not yet.

Was it even a real memory? And if false memories weren't inserted by evil therapists and hypnotists, as often alleged, where in fact did they come from? Anyway, evil therapists usually inserted memories of childhood abuse, and the train memory, while dripping with anxious feelings of abandonment, wasn't about abuse.

Sandrine felt tempted to haul a stepladder into the bedroom and unfold it under the trapdoor. She'd climb to the top step, tea in hand. It was the kind of minor eccentricity she liked to indulge in. She told people she was practicing for menopause. She'd even walked the streets of her village carrying a coffee mug, and not the stainless travel kind but a proper ceramic mug with daisies and ewes on it.

She looked at her husband meditatively chewing on his pencil end. All she had to do was ask. Was his name Ethan? Or maybe Karl Johann? If it wasn't either of those, then what was it? Maybe she'd written his name in one of her notebooks. In fact, that was highly likely.

Very quietly, so as not to disturb his chewing, she got up and tiptoed down the hall. The bedroom closet was capacious enough to hold large objects such as the stepladder in addition to their meagre supply of clothing. Leveraging the ladder out through a selection of her man's plaid shirts, she opened it beneath the pink trapdoor in the ceiling. The trapdoor was pink because Sandrine had once painted the walls and ceiling, rebelling against her husband's blues and browns and camo. It was his house; he'd inherited it along with two or three other nearby properties both large (a swampy hunt camp) and small (a cottage on one of the lakes), and every damn wall or floor or roof or exterior wall on or in each of his houses, sheds, and barns was either green or blue or brown. Sandrine remembered how when they'd begun dating she'd taken whatshisname for financially struggling because of his frayed shirts and ailing trucks. She was used to city signifiers of prosperity: clever phones and name brand clothing. His little white clapboard house near the Brookside canal, the one she'd moved into after they'd married, had been so unassuming she'd felt a little sorry for him. Later she'd found out it was a country thing; folks had houses and plots of swamp and cedar bush tucked away all over the county, bits and pieces that had been in the family for generations. Many families were cash poor but land rich, their various parcels having been acquired during earlier times when land had been cheap to come by, having then been recently expropriated from the local Mississauga. It was still cheap, comparatively speaking, tucked away in this forgotten Eastern Ontario township.

Sandrine stopped in mid-thought halfway up the ladder, imagining a house painted in camouflage. She smiled. It could be quite wonderful, certainly a talking point. Would she use the green-and-brown kind or the greyscale kind? The different types of camo had different names; Sandrine just didn't know what they were. What she did know was that she had once painted the bedroom not camo but a flaming flamingo pink. She'd done it when her husband was away hunting, just to prove that she had some say, to prove that pink was a good colour. If he hated pink so much he shouldn't have married a girl; a moose would've done just fine. Moose, after all, were brown.

Still parked halfway up, Sandrine pictured Mike's winsome moose wife and giggled. Then she climbed back down to retrieve the flashlight that always sat on her nightstand in case of a power failure; there were lots of those in the country, just as there was lots of camo. Truth was the pink had gotten to her, too—the much and suchness of it; maybe a paler pink would've done the trick just as well, proved the point, made her husband laugh instead of groan.

Once back at the top she pushed the trapdoor out of the way. It wasn't hinged, just a loose slab of wood squared a little irregularly to fit the slightly irregular square someone had long, long ago cut into the ceiling. Sandrine hoisted herself up and turned on the flashlight.

She'd bring the box of books down, she figured, or she'd sit up there all night, opening one book after another, trying to find the passage about the lozenges woven into or printed onto the train upholstery. If she were smart, once she'd found it she wouldn't slip the book, unlabelled, back into its box. She'd slap a sticky note on the page, or she'd get a fine-point marker and write on the cover, or she might even take the book and carry it down the ladder to keep on her night table until it drove her crazy and she could no longer stand the presence of this chapter from an earlier life, recorded in neat cursive hailing from the days before her handwriting had gone to hell.

Amazingly, the box was right near the hatch, as if someone had pushed it there for her perusal. Or else she'd had this same idea a month ago, and forgotten. Just like her husband's name.

She selected a book from the top layer, opened it in the middle and read aloud: *Over the course of a lifetime, I have found that random thoughts, like dreams, can be cryptic messages from the soul, disguised or veiled, yes, but requiring only a bit of personal pondering, inspection or introspection, to parse their meaning and significance.*

Not the passage about the lozenges, not at all, but maybe there was a connection nevertheless. For instance, hadn't she just been thinking that often enough the timing of certain thoughts was significant? Did that mean there was a reason she was thinking about the train in Africa on which her father had left her, promising to meet her in Tunis the next day while he went to visit an old French girlfriend living in the south, in Tataouine?

What happened, Sandrine? Did something happen on the train that you've shut out? Is that why you're thinking so much about the damn train suddenly? Djerba's other name was the Isle of

Forgetting, after all.

Or is it the feeling of abandonment by your father that you're still, decades later, trying to heal? Maybe nothing beyond his departure had to have happened for you to feel so neglected. Maybe the train voyage was perfectly innocent and nice, if a little bit frightening as you spoke neither Arabic nor French well, and Tunisia isn't the sort of country in which young teen girls travel alone, then or now.

Did something happen on the train, Sandrine? Think a little harder.

Maybe, like her husband's name, she'd written it down in one of the notebooks, whatever it was. There were so many books in the box. Layers and layers of books, not in any kind of order. She looked at the one she held in her hand with its green cover and creamy lined pages, not all of them full. She hated wasting journals. She could resume writing in this one, just to confuse the hell out of herself when, in another ten years, she got it out of the box so she could look for her husband's forgotten name again.

What was the point of even having a husband if you couldn't even remember his name from one moment to the next?

She closed the book again, looked at the cover, which all by itself ought to offer clues. Without perusing the interior, she ought to be able to discern both the approximate year and her place of residence at the time of writing. Maybe even where she'd gotten the journal itself, whether it had been a gift or something she'd purchased in a stationery store, unable to help herself, knowing she shouldn't, not really, because it was expensive and the rent was due.

She opened the book to a random page.

The café she is sitting in is like the café on 6th Street, she read. *That one was a basement café with nice white cups and healthy carrot bread. She would leave her apartment and walk there during the day. The clerks were supercilious. She felt her loneliness and her poverty were both recognized and snickered at, a little. She was cute enough and her thrift-store coat was of good wool and a becoming cut; with a church-sale silk scarf, she thought she looked quite good. And yet anyone must be able to tell that she was lonely and bored and aimless.*

Sandrine couldn't remember having written this, nor could she remember the café, but there had been a lot of those over a span beginning approximately at the time of the trip to Tunisia and ending when she moved into her husband's house and started a family. She never went to those sorts of cafés anymore, mainly because there weren't any in Brookside or Stony Creek, villages that favoured Canadian Chinese and breakfast specials. She examined the handwriting. It was undeniably her own, evoking the long-gone days before her cursive had gone to hell. She felt a little regretful looking at her beautiful penmanship, wondering whether she could relearn it. Trying to recover lost cursive would be sort of like going back to French or pottery, both skills she'd once been not half-bad at but had left by the wayside at some point.

Probably the same point at which she got pregnant, if not before. She'd taken up reading about nutrition and child development, consequently, both French verb conjugations and wheel throwing had seemingly vanished—poof!—from her brain as if they'd never been there at all.

Did it even matter? She wasn't with Mike or Randy or Euell or Darrel because of his name but because, with him, she no longer had to be that person, the one who scribbled obsessively in sad cafés, the one who had looked out the windows of a train that had seemed, forever, to pass through the North African night. On Djerba there were three-thousand-year-old olive trees, still living. What did trees that old dream of? An older dream than that of the Romans, by far.

What happened on the train, Sandrine?

She had in the end tired of the years of lonely views and

focused just on the upholstery, its patterns repeating, over and over. Clack clack clackety clack. Eventually, the train had left North Africa and gone back to Canada as only dream trains can.

Sandrine heard her husband enter the bedroom. She listened to him sit down on the bed; it must be late, even by her standards. She began her descent, clutching the little green hardcover book with its descriptions of thought processes and sad cafés, if not train upholstery. Later she'd leaf through it again and hopefully come across a list of lovers' names that would end with her husband's.

"The Dreams of Trees" originally appeared in the Bibliotheca Fantastica Anthology published by Dagan Books in 2013.

BILLY

Michael Mirolla

BILLY (A NAME HE INFINITELY prefers to the Guglielmo given him at birth) has one leg shorter than the other, the result of an unfortunate encounter with a public transport vehicle. The midwinter accident, leaving Billy trapped between the spinning back wheels and a hard-packed snow bank, couldn't have happened at a worst time. Billy was in the midst of undergoing some difficult hormonal changes and about to experience his first growth spurt. Although the spurt arrived on time, it only took hold of the upper half of his body, giving him the look of a bandy-legged, weightlifting rooster. And that, as a rule, could be more than ample reason for pity or derision. That could be the signal to take the luckless victim under society's wing, to relegate him to that area where "tut-tut" is the operative word most often heard. This is especially true when the person happens to be a second-generation immigrant. But no one sighs or laughs or "tut-tuts" when Billy ambles by, his misstep making it appear as if he can't decide what height he really wants to be. No one chooses to point him out with a wiggling finger or to express open sympathy with his plight. No one comments on his status as an abandoned youth or as one of life's incompletely formed. And certainly no one says that Billy should be in some sort of institution, at least no one says it out loud. No one says it in his presence. For, you see, any or all of the above options would hurt Billy's sensibilities and that, in turn, wouldn't be very healthy for those exercising said options.

Despite the asymmetry or because of it, Billy takes great pleasure in dressing in his finest duds and strolling the streets. "His" streets, having returned to claim uncontested ownership not long after his final graduation from the Shawbridge Farm and Reformatory School for Wayward Boys. Occasionally and for no particular reason, he stops, sticks his hands into his specially made silk trouser pockets and broods. More often, he simply concentrates on forcing himself not to smile, in keeping with his serious, if somewhat self-imposed, responsibilities. When he does choose to focus on someone, look out. It's as if the rifles from a firing squad had suddenly been primed. Some might be tempted to say that behind that hooded, lizard stare lies spread the deadly history of Park Extension, of misinterpreted New World dreams and rough woollen underwear that hasn't been changed quite often enough. Or that has been worn threadbare from too many direct applications of javel water. Some might be tempted to say that despite the fact Billy's own underwear is always of the finest weave and never has to be worn more than once. But no one would. And how Billy has managed to go from abandoned childhood to personal tailor is another question that's best left unexplored.

Billy cherishes his independence, his freedom to do as he pleases when he pleases. He lives by himself in a pleasant but modest two-room flat above an Armenian grocery store-cum-dentist office. This flat had once housed his mother as well but she opted out of the lease soon after Billy's accident (his father having opted out long before that, cursing the land repeatedly as the boat headed back to the Old Country). As far as anyone can tell, he has lived by himself ever since when, that is, not taking part in one of his sporadic reform school apprenticeships. And he has made it known, forcibly at times, that this is the condition he prefers, that he doesn't care for anyone and isn't interested in sharing the occasional heart-to-heart the rest of us find so soothing. Never has, never will. In fact, his favourite expression, and this from a young man of very few words, is: "I couldn't give a flying mother about youse. Get outta my face." Which freely translated means: Avoid the dapper gentleman for the foreseeable future or you won't have much of a future to foresee.

But only his "friends" does he treat in such a chivalrous and courtly manner. As for his enemies, they receive no warning. None whatsoever. Often, by the time they find out about their ill-fated change in status, it's too late. Way too late. One moment, they're walking along a sunset-cloaked Park Ex street, whistling with youthful exuberance and without a care in the world after a visit with an accommodating signorina; the next, they're laid out expeditiously and efficiently, contemplating the dizzy, eternal round of stars from a dark pool of their own vital fluid. At which point, Billy might lean down and offer a helping hand. He might deign to explain what brought on the "lesson" in the first place and why it was deemed necessary. Or he might not.

And God help anyone crazy enough to disturb the calm of what Billy sweetly refers to as "home away from home." That's the far-wall, facing-the-door booth at the Nero's Palace night club where he sits for hours on end surrounded by a revolving cast of his favourites (always male), each bringing in a tithe or a trinket from their far-flung business activities. Chances are said disturbers, by definition strangers to the area who don't know any better and haven't taken proper heed of the danger signals, will soon be flying through picture windows one step ahead of a shotgun blast.

On most occasions, Billy will take care to shoot well over their heads but there's no telling when he won't. No telling when he might feel compelled to lower his aim. And then calmly walk away, leaving enough money to cover the shattered pane and a round for those with the courage to have stuck it out.

But what Billy enjoys best, what brings a spark into the perennial dull of his eyes, is a punishment he reserves for only the most heinous of crimes: a punishment that involves jumping from the tops of fences. Fences not too high and not too low; fences with just the right footholds; fences with the proper give and take. And then landing with a delicious thud on the chest of his laid-out victim, pinned down below with uncaring yet casual effectiveness by Billy's Hounds.

Billy's Hounds are his ace retrievers. He, himself, due to the previously mentioned lack of symmetry, can't run with any competence. Besides, such precipitous motion would be a gross indignity, an admitting of undue haste and concern when those words don't exist in Billy's vocabulary. But his retrievers, also reform-school trained, are the finest in all of Park Ex. Always hungry, lithe, lean and long of limb, breathlessly swift and guaranteed not to injure the prey. In short, they're exemplary hounds, recruited with just one purpose in mind. Nothing can divert them or lead them astray: neither family loyalty nor "agenbites of inwit." A false trail, an attempt to dodge down some garbage-strewn alley, will most certainly prove useless: Billy's Hounds know every street, every dead-end, every abandoned building, garage and construction site in Park Ex. And a plea for mercy only excites them the more, only leads them to snigger and nod knowingly, all the while closing in with military precision. A sudden turn, a snarl, a show of teeth and knotted fists has the best effect causing them to stop in their tracks. But only for a moment. For they're quick to recover more fearful of returning empty-handed than of any damage the quarry might be able to inflict.

Once surrounded and caught, once made to understand there's no escape, once led to the point of no return (normally at the base of the chain-link metal fence that runs along the railroad track), the victim's waiting must be a terrible, excruciating agony. Billy's slow side-tilted gait becomes even more pronounced at such times. He will stop occasionally like a man in love to crack his knuckles. Or to suck on a minted toothpick. Or to comb his Brilliantined hair. Or to adjust the buttons on his dapper double-breasted suit. As he resumes his walk, a cold somewhat cynical moon gleams back from his newly shined footwear. For he always detours through the railroad station concession to have his boots polished to a sparkle before a "kill." And he smiles. Now he smiles. At last, he smiles. Such a smile is hard to imagine, quite impossible to re-create in any believable way. You need a dark soul, one never given a chance, a soul crushed beyond recognition under the relentless tires of a winter bus. And then you need to sprinkle this dark with just the right amount of emptiness, a little soupçon of nothing like the cursed wake of a retreating ghost ship.

Following the jingle up the chain-link fence (not too high, not too low), Billy's downward flight is a thing of infinite beauty, of perfect arc, of ultra-accurate trajectory: a rainbow with every single colour rubbed out save the red. It's all the more fascinating in that, on the way down, one boot is necessarily ahead of the other for a double thunk. A thu-thunk. And, if you listen carefully enough, if you put your mind to it, you can hear Billy's delighted "wheeee!" as he allows gravity to mete out justice for him. Only once has he missed beneath the shadow of that concrete overpass into Park Ex and that was definitely towards excess. With a crushed skull, a careering ambulance ride, a critical listing the result.

It's only after such punishments that Billy allows himself a few laughs, that Billy lets his guard down. Then in the familiar surroundings of his "home" and circumscribed by his faithful

Hounds, each one vying for a pat on the head or a word of praise he opens up and begins to talk. What's more, he allows others to talk, those with infinitely better verbal skills and memories, those with a gift for gab. For Billy isn't afraid to admit his own deficiencies when it comes to such matters as long as no one else does. The talk is of exploits and brave deeds, of the good old days at the reform school, of escapes attempted and escapes succeeded. Anything goes, provided the evening ends with a recap of Billy's own accomplishments and a reaffirming of his value to the community.

But one mustn't get the impression Billy's life is all peaches and cream, all sweetness and light. Sometimes his enemies, envious of his success, will stage a pre-emptive strike deep into his staked-out territory, causing havoc among Billy's business associates and appropriating their hard-earned goods. Sometimes, emboldened by grief or blinded by revenge, the brother or the cousin or the long-time friend of the crushed skull will blast away the picture window of Billy's "home" and then retreat to the far side of the railroad overpass, safe in the womb of another language, another night. And sometimes, there's even a certain tit-for-tat, with one of Billy's Hounds tossed off the same railroad bridge to scream and flail and suffer a shattered spine on the unforgiving tracks below.

On such occasions, there's no talking to Billy. No point in even trying. A pure madness invades his eyes. It's a clean devoid-of-life madness. It's a madness that allows him to stash a machine-gun under his spotless, recently dry-cleaned trench coat. That allows him to stand vigil all night over "his" end of the bridge, the one necessary gap in an otherwise impenetrable armour. No doubt dangerous and exposed, if someone doesn't know his enemies. But Billy knows them intimately, knows them as he knows himself. Better, really. For he's had plenty of occasion to deal with them.

Come on, he will say, legs apart and well-balanced, machine-gun held loosely in one hand. Come to me, youse bleeding mothers, he will say while his Hounds wait curled up and whimpering at the base of the overpass. Come on. Here I am. Come and get me. And, unable to help themselves, his enemies will begin their long sojourn from the well-guarded halls of warmth and protection, from the arms of their girlfriends, from the pool room basements full of dusty light, from the 24-hour snack bars redolent with the smell of vinegar and ketchup. Clomp, clomp, clomp, marching in orderly phalanxes up the cement ramp, up the crumbling steps, drawn by the absolute magnet of Billy's hate. They march and they fall, blown away by the steady blissful rat-a-tat that blazes like a single red-hot eye from somewhere close to Billy's heart.

And then they march and they fall again and again after that, the entire night long. And for every single night after that. Tireless. Unconcerned with the niceties of time and plans for the future. They march and fall again as often as Billy calls them and that could be a long, long time.

You see, neither simple death nor the promise of subsequent resurrection is enough for Billy. It has never been enough. Not nearly enough.

It's the again and again that comes closest to satisfying his soul. It's the stiff blast of eternity he seeks out. A relentless pursuit for release.

In the fervent hope that, someday, his enemies will do the same for him.

SPOILED RICE

Sang Kim

ALL THREE OF US WERE RIDING in the front seat of our Big Uncle's sunny Chrysler Cordoba. Uncle had left it for Father before moving his family back to Korea. Things were beginning to look up over there, he said. The car came in handy because Father now drove to his warehouse job instead of taking the 24-hour bus. Sister made big loopy waves out the window and when the wind nearly ripped her arm from her shoulder, she squealed like a pig. We were heading for a motel near the airport where Father said a woman there would take care of us now that Mother was gone and where Family Services couldn't find us.

The last time FS came for Father, he didn't put up a fight, so the cops didn't have to throw him to the pavement and take out the cuffs. That was a Saturday, and the snot-nosed kids from the project stopped playing basketball and came around Trayvon's front yard to stare and kiss their teeth. Upstairs, a woman in a grey suit spoke in a low voice to Mother, who had locked herself up in the bathroom to put some powder on her face. When Father returned from the police station that night, he cried under Mother's bedroom window, going on about how sorry he was for hitting her and promising to never touch her or the bottle again. And for a time he kept his word until dumb Mother let slip about that man at the textile factory again. Father was back into the fridge for beer, then on to the basement for his stash of home-made rice wine. His voice always sounded a little different when he came up from down there.

This time around, Mother was preparing dinner. You could always tell what type of mood she was in by the way she washed the rice. When she was happy, she held the edge of the pot with both hands like a steering wheel and swirled it in a gentle circular motion and drained the cloudy water into the sink four times. After soaking it in cold water for exactly fifteen minutes, she would place the pot in the rice cooker and turn it on. Sometimes, she washed the rice like she lost something valuable, making slow figure eights in the pot with one hand while singing songs from the old world. Sad stuff about a boy who left the village and was supposed to return to his girl after making some money but stayed on with the town's tramp. When she was angry, you could see the white knuckles of one hand gripping the pot's rim, and the other clenched into a fist, kneading the rice like the way that fat man worked the dough at the pizza joint. You could hear the grains cracking. Mother told us cracked grains made the rice taste sour, but she never told us why. All I knew was that our rice was different from the one Trayvon and his family ate. Theirs was long and brown, with mushy beans in it. Different too from the rice that Deepak brought to school, which looked like toenail clippings and smelled even worse. Our rice was soft and pearly and just sticky enough for a perfect mound to be picked up with our chopsticks and shovelled into our mouths. When it was done just right, there was always a touch of something sweet in it.

Sister and I were on our pull-out sofa bed in the living room, watching *Fantasy Island*. Our favourite scene was on when that man-child rings the bell in the tower and points to a plane in the sky to announce its arrival. We stood on the bed, pointed to our water-stained ceiling, and shouted, "Zee plane! Zee plane!" It was then that Father stomped up the stairs and into the kitchen. He yelled at Mother, but I couldn't make anything out. I was trying to listen to what the tall man in the white suit was saying to the little man as people were getting off the plane. And Sister was stuttering, like she always does when things get a bit heavy around the house or when she is on the floor at church filled with the Holy Ghost and the spit's coming out of her mouth. After Father punched the second hole through the kitchen wall, Mother calmly wiped her hands on her apron and went upstairs. She came back down with a suitcase and her lips all done up the same colour as her ruby red dress, wiped my crybaby sister's mouth with her hand, and told us that she was going to visit a friend for a few days. You watch over her, she mouthed to me from the back door.

THE MOTEL WAS IN A STRIP PLAZA with a bar on one end and an empty swimming pool on the other. There was brown slime along the rim of the pool and dead leaves bunched up in the deep end. Father parked the car right in front of our unit. Across the parking lot, there was an arcade, tanning salon, and an adult video store. Our room smelled like an ashtray, and a greasy curtain covered a small window facing the airport runway on the other side of a barb-wired fence. Every few minutes, a plane took off. It felt a lot like Pastor Kwan's descriptions of the end of the world when the ground rumbles and tears apart and sucks all the sinners down into it.

"I like it here," Sister said, jumping up and down on the bed. "Are we staying long?" Father sat on the edge of the other bed and lit a cigarette.

"Until Mother comes back," he said. His voice was returning to normal again. Someone knocked on the door and Father stubbed out his cigarette quickly before he went to open it. A woman stood there, held Father's face in her hands, then turned to us with a smile. She wore a long brown skirt and shoes that were flat and not shiny with high heels like the ones Mother put on whenever Father worked his Friday night shift. And her eyes were different from Mother's, too—big and soft with none of that dried clumpy mascara stuff. Those eyes reminded me of the card I received from my grade four teacher last Christmas with a painting of oil lamps burning inside two rooms of a house during a snowstorm.

"Hi Kyung Hee," she said. She knelt in front of Sister and offered her some rice rolls, which she took like a scaredy-cat. "So pretty now." She stroked Sister's head. Then she looked over to me. "Yong Su, you've grown into such a big handsome young man." I could tell my cheeks were getting that way when I did something embarrassing and people saw it. Nobody, except Mother and Father, called us by our Korean names, so hearing it come out of this woman's mouth made me feel strange even though it was said in such a warm way. I straightened my back and bowed my head slightly, the way Father always taught me, and said thank you.

"Mrs. Chung will be here to take care of you for a few days while I am at work," Father said. She stood there, holding her purse with both hands in front of her skirt and nodded her head. She looked around the room as though the walls and dresser and TV reminded her of something nice that happened to her recently. Father reached into his pants pocket and pulled out a bunch of coins.

"Take your sister to the arcade," he said. "Mrs. Chung and I need some time to talk." In front of the tanning salon, next to the arcade, a man in a white suit stood near the entrance smoking a cigarette. It was not like the ones Father smoked, which were short and stubby, or the ones Mother hid under the backyard porch that tasted like mint leaves. His was slim and brown with a plastic filter. He looked like he had spent too much time in the sun and was as wrinkly as raisins around his eyes. When he smiled at us his teeth were so shiny that I forgot to smile back. When we walked past him, I could feel his eyes burning holes into our backs.

The arcade was full of white kids. I could tell they played a lot of hooky and put their hands up girls' skirts whenever they felt like it. They turned and eyeballed us when we entered. The manager, with big pits on his nose, looked at us over his newspaper. "You kids are too young to be in here. I'll let it go this time because you're probably visiting from somewheres else. But don't be calling the cops on me." He snorted and flipped open the newspaper. "They probably didn't understand a thing," he said to the white kids, who turned back to their pinball machines. Sister played Ms. Pacman and I played Donkey Kong. I never got the Donkey part because there was never anything that looked like one in the game. I was good in the early stages, where I only had to jump over barrels and climb ladders to rescue the girl that Kong takes hostage. When we were down to our last coins, I told Sister to stay put, that I was going to ask Father for more. Halfway across the parking lot, I heard sounds coming from our room, like the ones Mother made when she let Father back into her bedroom sometimes. The door was slightly open with the chain holding it in place, so I could only see into part of the room. Mrs. Chung's skirt was crumpled up on the floor. It reminded me of a dead animal on the side of a highway. On the bed, I could make out her bare back, wet and slightly arched like she was trying to touch her chin to the ceiling. She was moving up and down slowly, the same way my sister rode the coin-operated horse at Galleria Mall. A foot stuck out of the blanket behind her. I knew it was Father's because of the nasty gash on it—a souvenir, he said, from stepping on an explosive when he was hunting the Commies who killed his parents. As I stood there, I knew better than to knock on the door and ask for more change. If I did, I thought something awful would come out of it—a kind of shadow might fall over everything in our lives, one that could never be erased. So I just turned back and returned to the arcade.

The white kids were cheering on some guy with fingerless leather gloves break the record on Asteroids. Sister was sitting on a bench by herself in the corner. When she said she was tired and hungry, I told her I was going to stick around and that she should go back by herself. I walked her out to the curb and watched her cross the parking lot. Father came to the door. He had on his pants and a white sleeveless undershirt. She said something to him and he looked my way. I couldn't tell if Mrs. Chung was still inside or not, but at that moment, for reasons I couldn't quite understand, I was happy for Sister. They went inside, leaving the door open for me.

When the arcade manager told all of us to scram because it was time to lock up, me and the white kids spilled outside together. Nobody said anything to me, and the kid with the fingerless gloves talked about getting some weed and going over to his place. I stood there in front of the blinking neon sign and watched them turn the corner. The door to our room was closed now and the lights were out. I didn't feel like going inside just yet, so I wandered over to the swimming pool, squeezed through an opening in the fence, and sat with my legs dangling over the deep end. There was a rumble like a thousand Kongs running to my left, then a loud whooshing sound. I looked up at a plane lifting off the runway. It was so close I could make out the outlines of passengers looking out of the small yellow windows. I wondered if they could see me sitting there at the pool. I remembered Mother saying once after the FS people left that someday she was going to take Sister and me to a better place on one of those big jets. I thought about where this plane might be going and if it was to a better place and whether or not Mother was on it without us.

THE REST OF THE TIME at the motel was a blur. Mrs. Chung came and went, but I never found out what happened to her afterwards. When we returned home five days later, the house was filled with the stench of something rotting. Father went into the kitchen, picked up the pot of rice from off the counter, and dumped it out in the backyard. He swore under his breath. Sister pinched her nose and opened the windows and doors. I went upstairs and opened the door to Mother's bedroom. She had taken all of her clothes off the hangers in the closet and her lipstick was lying on the night table, still open and cracking.

That night, after Sister fell asleep, I stepped out into the yard. The air was sticky and the sky was full of clouds with the moon hidden behind one of them. A million ants were crawling all over the mound of rice. Some of the grains were being carried away, one at a time, and in the flimsy light, they looked liked maggots moving along the grass. In the distance, a plane was headed in the direction of the airport, but there was something about it that didn't seem right. It was leaning too much to one side. I thought about the people inside and how scared they might be. When it looked like the plane was going to be okay, I lifted my arm and pointed my finger toward it, but nothing would come out of my mouth. At that moment, I felt like the little man on *Fantasy Island* who could never look eye-to-eye with anyone except some bratty child he had to watch over. Like him, maybe I would never grow any more than I already had and for the rest of my life I might always be looking up at the adult world around me, and even past it sometimes, adjusting my eyes to catch a bit of whatever good might come down from the sky.

MAI'S STORY

Caroline Vu

MY NAME IS MAI. Patients call me Dr. Luu. Between you and me, let's keep it simple. Please, no 'Doctor Luu,' just Mai. A young Mai from Hue, alone in Palawan—this is how I still see myself. This is why I am back here.

I knew Palawan a long time ago—as in another life, as in last year's bad dream. I remember the fine white sand beach. I remember the rows of identical tents. I remember odours from the latrines carried by the wind to overpower the smell of the sea. I remember so much yet I remember nothing. No coherent story despite all the details. Stories, I've waited so long to collect them, Sister. Please, let me hear them.

Stories. My mother never told me any as a child. In fact, she never said much to me besides "Do this" or "Do that." When she was expansive, it would be: "Why are you always slouching?" Early I learned to stay out of trouble by staying away from her.

The night we left Hue in a hurry, my mother said even less. All I heard that night was the occasional "Left," "Right" to guide me along a dark silent path. For hours we walked until my feet bled. After much pleading, we stopped to apply grass to my wounds. Then we walked some more.

Silence was all around us. It was not the soothing calm of rural roads—not that I knew anything about the countryside. No, it was the imposed quietness of curfews. The deceiving hours of tranquillity before the fall of rockets. This was the only type of silence I knew.

The night we left Hue furtively, we were dressed in torn pyjamas—the kind used to scrub kitchen floors. Our faces also got the same dirty treatment to better hide us in the darkness. Or was it to better mask our true roots? After years of propaganda, I knew well my guilt. I erred by going to school while others fought battles. Reading books while others tilled fields—this was my greatest error. "Counter-revolutionary" was a term stuffed so deep down my throat, I could only swallow it whole. Spitting it out was not an option.

The night we left long-suffering Hue—tragic like all the songs written about it—the light was still shining on the cathedral. I could still see its black spire slanting to the left. This spire was a point of reference. It had never failed me. Thanks to it, I've never gotten lost in all my years of running errands for my mother. Even during the worst days of the war, when ruined buildings made neighbourhoods unrecognizable, the cathedral's spire had shown me the way home. But on this particular night getting out of Vietnam, I was lost. Hopelessly lost.

When I saw the boat, my heart sank. It was small, crowded and derelict. Before I could protest, my mother grabbed my wrist to lead me on. In the excitement of the moment, my feet kept running. The salty water stung the open sores on my toes. I wanted to slow down. My mother wanted to hurry on. Only after reaching the rickety boat did my mother let go of my wrist. We boarded the vessel in our usual silence. I didn't tell her that I couldn't swim.

She already knew that. A hundred thoughts ricocheted in my head—unanswered questions, worries, dreams. Like my mother, I couldn't utter a single word.

The night we left Hue on a bobbing boat, I was still reluctant to intrude on my mother's silent world. In fact, I'd become immune to her absence of speech. With the years, her lack of answers to my questions no longer mattered. I just let it be. I knew not our destination. I knew nothing about our shipmates, our captain. Yet I did not ask, did not question my mother's judgment. On the overcrowded boat, I sat squeezed between strangers, using my saffron coloured cloth sack as a pillow. My conical hat, pressed against my chest, protected me from the wind. I closed my eyes and imagined the coming and going of foaming waves. I so wanted to block out the sobbing sounds of little children.

At some point during our moonless trip, my mother left me. Too preoccupied with seasickness, no one had noticed her disappearance. Nobody remembered a drowning. In fact, nobody remembered us—a middle-aged woman with a young girl. "We are large families with six, seven kids each," they'd all reported. "No single mother with only one child here," they'd said. "What about me? I'm here," I'd pleaded. To this, the people only shrugged their shoulders.

When I realized my mother wasn't with me on the boat, I panicked. I looked for her familiar bulging eyes amongst the other refugees and found only blank stares. I searched the boat's nooks and crannies for her brown chequered backpack but found only human waste that nobody bothered to clean. I looked over the boat's railing and saw the South China Sea at its best—quietly rippling. There wasn't a shark or a body in sight.

The other children laughed at my tears. When not throwing up in their mother's arms, they'd show me their clenched fists. Or they'd stick their tongues at me. My misery had somehow calmed their queasy stomachs.

One month after leaving Hue, I ended up in Palawan, a refugee camp in the Philippines. Somehow, somewhere on the open sea, I'd become an orphan. I had no proof of my mother's death or drowning. Her body never washed up on the fine white sand of Palawan. I wasn't even sure if she'd managed to board the boat with me that moonless night so long ago. I will never know. My days of abandonment were spent transforming banana leaves into hats. This kept me busy while languorously time ticked on. I was hot. I remember the scorching sun sucking drops of sweat from my skin. I remember the unrelenting humidity teasing my hair. I remember getting official recognition from the UN High Commission for Refugees. I had become a "real" orphan in their eyes. With such a status, I soon found myself sponsored by a Canadian church. In Guelph, I became a local poster girl. As a poor, homeless orphan, I made people feel good about their charitable donations. And I wallowed in the pity everyone sent me.

What happened on the boat? I had been asked and asked myself a thousand times. Did my mother board the boat with me? Probably. Did she drown? Probably not. Was she robbed, killed and thrown overboard? No. I must admit I didn't see any of that. Then again, my memory of those days remained as foggy as a damp autumn night. With the years, I have forgotten my experience of fleeing Vietnam as a young girl. "The night I left Hue furtively dressed in torn pyjamas . . ." is a story I often tell friends curious about my past. They don't know that narrative is full of holes plugged by an imagination mediocre at best.

Palawan. Why am I here again? Why did I return to this treeless, stinky refugee camp that was my first home away from home? For the stories, Sister. I am here to collect stories. I am here to see with my own eyes young children searching for their lost parents. I am here to meet girls who had betrayed their past to become someone else. Perhaps then, I will remember my own tale.

Sister, if you write my story, my mother might see it one day.

Then she'd realize that I'm still thinking of her. I haven't given up hope of finding her. She'd reckon that I am still sitting on the saffron-coloured cloth sack she'd sewn for me years ago. It is now a prized pillow in my fancy living room. She'd see that all my hard work was for her. Maybe she'd smile at my diploma. Perhaps she'd even utter a few words: " My daughter, Dr. Luu . . ." Even if she'd nothing to say, I want her to know her silence still speaks to me. This is my only wish. Please write this story, Sister.

THE SCENT OF LEMONS

Ian Thomas Shaw

G ABRIELLA NOTICES HIM AGAIN AS she squeezes the lemons for the Amaretto Sours that the tourists love so much. They had only put out the Help Wanted sign that morning but four times he has passed by and she wonders if he's interested. They could use the help. Soon the holiday-goers will be flocking to Polignano a Mare. Why doesn't he just come inside and ask for work? He walks by again but doesn't stop. His complexion is dark, darker than hers. His high cheekbones and angular jaw speak to their common ancestry. She pours the squeezed lemon juice into a bottle then breathes in its scent before putting it into the refrigerator. The door opens.

He is standing there, somewhat confused but with a definite look of hunger. Maybe he has just come for a handout, something to tide him over until he finds work. Gabriella starts to take a day-old loaf from the pantry. They keep it there for the *senzatetto*—the homeless. She feels her Uncle Salvatore's hand on her wrist. "I will talk to him," he says. Her uncle strolls over to the young man.

"*Prego*." He motions him inside, but the young man just stands there. Uncle Salvatore points to the sign and turns his hand to ask if this is why he is here. The young man nods.

"Do you speak Italian?" asks her uncle, but the young man looks at him blankly. "Do you speak Tigrinya?" her uncle then asks. Gabriella is surprised. She had forgotten that her uncle spoke the Eritrean language. But of course he did. Though Italian, he had spent his childhood in Asmara, long before she was born, and had returned to work there many years later. It was there he had met her Aunt Asmeret. When things started to collapse in Eritrea, he brought all of them to Italy. Her mother had always told her that he had saved them, and Gabriella grew up to love and respect her Uncle Salvatore, whose easy going manners were so different from those of her Aunt Asmeret and mother. Whenever Gabriella hurt herself playing, it was Uncle Salvatore who would rescue her from the two women's scolding. Sometimes, he would even bring her a gelato despite the women's warnings that he was spoiling her.

The young man looks up and asks something in Tigrinya that Gabriella doesn't catch. Her uncle lowers his voice and continues to speak to the young man in broken Tigrinya. Gabriella only understands a word or two. Since coming to Italy, she has hardly spoken the language. She feels shame that she no longer masters her own language. A sense of embarrassment also emerges that she never uses her birth name in Italy. Here she is Gabriella, only Gabriella. No one calls her Zula anymore, not her aunt, not even her mother. "What is wrong with Zula," she once asked her mother. "It doesn't sound right in Italian," her mother answered. "You want to fit in here, don't you?"

She hears her uncle speaking to her.

"Gabriella, call your Aunt Asmeret and ask her to come down here."

She obeys immediately and punches into her cell phone the number to the upstairs apartment.

"*Pronto.*"

"Auntie, we have a young man in the café who doesn't speak Italian. I think that he is Eritrean. Uncle Salvatore would like you to come down."

"I'll be right there."

Uncle Salvatore has seated the young man at the bar and is preparing an espresso for him. With hand gestures, he asks him if he wants something to eat. The young man raises his hands to show he has no money. Uncle Salvatore wags his finger and clicks his tongue to say, "It doesn't matter." He pulls out some white bread and goat cheese and makes the young man a simple sandwich. The young man's hands shake as he accepts the sandwich. Slowly, he says *grazie* and Uncle Salvatore pats him on the back, "*Bene.* Good you speak a little Italian." Gabriella hears her Aunt Asmeret scurrying down from the upstairs apartment. When she sees the young man, she raises her hand to her mouth and sinks into a chair.

"*Zia*—Auntie, what is it?"

"It's . . . it's just that for a moment I thought I saw a ghost."

"A ghost?"

"Yes, that young man looks so much like Tesfay."

"Do you mean my father?"

"Yes, your father."

Gabriella tries to conjure up the image of the father she has never known. The army had forcibly conscripted him to fight in the war against Ethiopia. That was shortly after she was born, and he never returned. She looks at her aunt and senses the pain of re-opening this old wound. The young man is staring at them now. He seems to have lost his nervousness. Aunt Asmeret approaches him, and they begin to speak in Tigrinya. After a while, Asmeret rises up, walks to Salvatore and speaks to him quickly in Italian. Her uncle nods and goes back to the kitchen, returning this time with an apron.

The café has begun to fill up with its regular patrons. Gabriella attends to them and loses sight of the young man, who disappears into the kitchen. Her aunt comes over to help her.

"Who is he?" asks Gabriella.

"Never mind," says her aunt. "He will work here awhile, but I want you to stay away from him."

"Why?"

"Just do what I ask."

Gabriella sees in her aunt's face a determination to assert her authority. It doesn't matter. This young man won't be around for long, but she wonders why she can't simply talk to him.

THE WEEK IS BUSY. Foreign tourists now fill the café and attempt their awful Italian on Gabriella. Most of them are German. She doesn't like Germans. Too tall and blond. They remind her of the ultra-right nationalists in Milan who swore at her when she started university there last fall. She is happy to be working in Polignano for the summer and away from her mother, who is living in Rome with her new boyfriend. The townspeople here know her well and treat her with respect. And for them, she is just another Italian. In Milan, she is a foreigner and alone.

"Can we get those cappuccinos?" a young German asks gruffly. She hates the impatience of these tourists. She knows that they are essential to the economy of the resort towns on the Adriatic, but she can't stand their arrogance. And today, she is overwhelmed by all the orders. Suddenly, the young man appears by her side and takes the freshly poured cappuccinos from her and carries them over to the table of Germans. She turns to a customer who is patiently waiting to pay her bill.

"Don't worry, little one, you can never work fast enough for those Germans," says the woman with a smile. "I know. I worked in Germany for five years."

Gabriella smiles at the woman.

"It is good that you've come back to help your aunt this summer. We don't have many young people left in Polignano to do the work. And is that your brother?"

"My brother? No. I don't really know him. He just started working with us this week."

"He is *un bel ragazzo*, isn't he?"

A beautiful boy? Gabriella hadn't thought of that. She looks at the young man, who is returning to the counter with the money the Germans have given him. She looks into his eyes. They sear through her. She blushes and remembers her aunt's warning.

"*Un ragazzo molto bello,*" utters the woman customer as she pats Gabriella's hand.

THE REST OF THE WEEK passes quickly. She learns from her aunt that the young man is called Jemal. He is one of the many refugees now flooding into Italy. He doesn't have any identity papers, so Uncle Salvatore is paying him under the table and has arranged a cot in the kitchen for him. Gabriella likes Jemal. He is polite and hard-working but hardly ever smiles. She asks her aunt to teach her more Tigrinya so she can talk to Jemal, but Asmeret firmly says no. She warns Gabriella to keep her distance. Gabriella is taken back by her aunt's attitude. Is it because Jemal is a Muslim? She has rarely seen her aunt attend mass and her uncle, Salvatore, is an atheist and Communist. She doesn't want to disobey her aunt, but she wonders if there is not something more.

Perhaps, it is the thrill of thinking to do something forbidden. Perhaps, it is because it is the first time in her life she has met a young man like her. Well, not quite like her but different enough from the Italian boys she has known. She begins to watch Jemal. He is graceful in his movements. His eyes are attentive and respectful. He never stares at her like the Italian boys do. Yet she thinks, at least she wants to think, that he likes her. She begins to dream at night what it would feel like to have his dark skin pressed against her, to hear him whisper her name, Zula, and tell her about her homeland. Gradually, these nocturnal fantasies become her daydreams too, and she can't help but think of him as she hums the sweet Eritrean melodies her grandmother taught her as a child. She hasn't forgotten everything, and this makes her happy. She notices that Jemal looks up each time she tries to sing the lyrics to the songs, and it makes him smile. He smiles even more when she stops halfway through a melody that she always forgets the ending to. She tries to learn from her aunt the second part of the song, but Asmeret feigns ignorance. Gabriella doesn't believe her.

She knows her aunt has been in touch with her mother. There is talk that her mother will soon visit Polignano. She begins to resent her aunt's obstinacy, her petty prejudices. She knows though that her mother is even more conservative and so proud to have become Italian. So proud that she stopped speaking Tigrinya many years ago. And now she is talking about marrying her new boyfriend and taking his Italian name. She wants Gabriella also to take his name too. Moretti—such a common name. Such a common man. No, she will not take that name. Since Jemal arrived, memories of her childhood have returned—playing in the dirt courtyard, picking lemons with her grandmother, the intense heat of the Asmara sun . . . And when her uncle and aunt are not watching, she catches Jemal's attention and points to herself, mouthing her name, Zula, I am Zula. The young man turns away but not before raising his fingers to send a shy greeting.

JEMAL ALWAYS RISES EARLY in the morning. Most days, she can hear him cleaning the café, hours before it opens. She wonders if he ever sleeps. She is always tempted to sit on the stairs and watch him work, but she knows that would cause her problems so she lays back in her bed and just listens. Sometimes, he is humming the same melodies that she does. It is as if they are two birds chirping mating calls to each other. She wonders, does he like her?

Does he love her? Finally, she tries to speak to him in the café. She has been online to learn a few more key phrases in Tigrinya. He is out back emptying the garbage cans. They only have a minute. She tells her uncle that she needs something from the kitchen and asks him to tend the bar. She straightens her dress, the one with roses on a cream background, which makes the darkness of her skin stand out. She wants to be like him, like the burnt earth of her grandmother's orchard. Jemal is straightening up the garbage cans that the cats have knocked over. She wants to walk up to him unannounced, touch his shoulder. Perhaps then he will understand.

"Gabriella, come here!" The voice of her aunt rings out, she looks up at her in the window above. Jemal turns around too. His face expresses no surprise but he isn't smiling either. But she smiles at him. "Gabriella?" The voice is now louder. "Yes, I'm coming." She flutters her fingers in a secret wave at Jemal and re-enters the café.

TODAY IS SUNDAY, THE CAFÉ will be closed until after the morning mass—no need to rise early. But she hears several voices downstairs. She looks out the window. The sun has not even risen. The voices grow louder and more urgent. She quickly dresses and walks to the top of the stairs. She can hear her uncle speaking in Italian and then in his broken Tigrinya. She also hears Mr. Gambini, the town's mayor, but can't make out what he is saying. A hand on her shoulder startles her. She turns to see her aunt's stern face. Uttering apologies, Gabriella returns to her bedroom.

Gabriella awakes to the ringing of her alarm clock. It is eight o'clock and time to prepare breakfast. She hopes that this Sunday, her aunt will go to mass and leave her alone to talk to Jemal. She sneaks by her aunt's bedroom. She is still sleeping. Gabriella tiptoes down the stairs. Uncle Salvatore is at the till, counting out money. Jemal sits silently in a chair. Her uncle hands Jemal some money, the week's wages. No, it looks like much more than that.

The young man stands up, pulls his knapsack onto his shoulder and readies to leave. Her uncle embraces Jemal and pats him on the back.

"Uncle, what's happening. Why is Jemal leaving? Is this because of me? That is unfair! It's not right!"

"No, it's not because of you. The Carabinieri are searching the town for illegal migrants."

"So that's it? You are just sending him away like that?"

"Don't worry, he will be fine. He's made it this far, hasn't he?"

"Where is he going?"

"To Germany. There is plenty of work there, and the German government is giving asylum to everyone."

"He should stay. He will be treated better here."

She can see that Jemal is trying hard to understand what they are saying but can't. Finally, he shakes her uncle's hand and turns to her. He takes her hand in his and says, "*Grazie, molto grazie*." Gabriella freezes as the young man walks to the door and gently opens it. He looks back and sings the final stanza of the Eritrean melody that she always forgets, then vanishes into the street. For a moment she's unsure what to do. Tears blur her vision. She wants to run into the streets to find him, but her feet refuse to move. She feels her uncle's firm grip on her shoulders and calms into silent obedience.

The commotion has woken her Aunt Asmeret who is watching from the stairs. She comes over to Gabriella and whispers in her ear, "'The Scent of Lemons.' It is such a beautiful song. Your father used to sing it to us."

"Auntie, what! So you do know the song?"

"Yes, Zula, now I will teach it to you," Asmeret murmurs in Tigrinya.

She squeezes her aunt's hand. Her uncle preps the espresso machine. Her tears dry. The church bells announce a new day in Polignano a Mare, and in faraway Asmara, young girls play under the lemon trees.

THE LONG WALK

Timothy Niedermann

—Bob, hang up the phone.

It's the same tone I always use. I practice it. Not loud, but firm. And definitely not conversational. No response necessary.

—Sorry, I'll have to call you back. Something's come up.

Bob puts his phone down and looks up at me from his desk.

—Hi, Steve.

They know what my job is, at least a part of it. So when I show up in person, it's not some petty detail of their billable hours or travel expenses I want to talk about. It's a pain in the ass, really. Firing people.

I'm still low on a very tall totem pole, so shit jobs naturally come my way. It's been almost two years, so I'll get promoted out of this soon enough. I'd better anyway. On the other hand, it's good corporate experience, learning how things work under the hood. Stuff to store in the back of my mind for later. But for now, it's part of the job.

—Bob, I'm sorry. You've been terminated. I'll need to take

your entry card, company credit card, cell phone, and laptop. Standard operating procedure. You know.

He sits still for a few moments, looking at me as if there's an explanation to be found somewhere on my face. His mouth opens just a bit, then closes. He knows there is nothing he can say. The deed is done. There is no appeal.

I let him sit there a little longer.

I know Bob slightly, worked with him on a couple of deals when I first joined the company. He was my superior then. Still is, actually. Nice guy. Talked a lot about his kids. Always in before nine, leaves most days a little after five, just like the rest of us.

Bob is—was—in marketing, like me, like most everybody here, it seems. Making presentations, talking to people, getting them to buy what the company sells. On the phone all day. Whom did Bob talk to? The same people always? You could count on that once. Build a relationship with a client, keep it for years. Nurture the relationship. Have lunch every so often. Get the best deal because you know each other, trust each other. Bob was good at his job. I learned a lot from him.

Normally—that is, according to the corporate handbook—Bob should have been called into the boss's office and given the bad news in person, by the one who made the decision. It was traditional. So, strictly speaking, my boss should be the one doing this—he is in charge of both of us—but the task got delegated to me. The man is busy, too busy for something you can't bill for. He likes to say "Time is money," meaning the lower pay grades should do the shit work. So no face-to-face with him for Bob today. That's the way it is.

The company is moving forward. There was a change of management a couple of years ago, just as I was applying for jobs out of school. I saw a dream opportunity—to grow in a dynamic environment with an exciting new corporate vision. And it's been great. Young people like me getting involved, putting in the hours.

Achieving results. The quarterlies are looking good now. Yeah!

The company has a good structure for advancement, too, one I was sure I could thrive in. They pay well and pay more as you prove your worth. I like marketing, using my main talent—the gift of the gab. But with substance. Really. The product is good. It has to be—or at least better than the competition's. And it's been fun. Met a lot of people. Sold lots of product.

A great professional experience so far.

Finally, Bob exhales and nods, then closes his laptop. It makes a small click. The overture to the usual music. He reaches back to take out his wallet from his back pocket and opens it flat right in front of him. He slides out the entry card and the credit card in turn, each making a sharp slap when he places it on the desk's surface. The cell phone makes a grating sound as he pushes slowly toward the laptop. The crescendo. Then silence.

—You'll need to sign these.

I hand him several short documents. The termination papers. He places them on the desk and lowers his head to read. He reads them as if they were any other business document—carefully, thoroughly.

This is Bob all right. Fastidious, deliberate. Never in a rush. He's a type. A true company man. A lifer.

A lifer. Not too many of those around anymore. Now it's up or out, and, as often as not, up and out to better pay and a fancier title somewhere else. That's the way things work. The market rules. Play the game. Only remember there's no ref, just a boss wanting to use you to look good. And make money for himself. Duh! The idea is to get to where he is and get some of that money for yours truly. Getting to that place, that's the real measure of a man, of success.

When Bob finishes the first document, he takes out a pen from his jacket pocket and signs and dates it where I have attached coloured plastic Post-it flags. Keeping the pen in his hand, he reads the rest and signs them each in turn. When he is done, he puts his pen back into his jacket pocket and pats the documents together. He lifts them up and taps the lower edges on his desk to align them, then hands them back to me.

—Here you go.

I take the documents and check the signature pages. Everything is in order.

—Your exit interview will be next Monday, at ten a.m. in conference room 205. Until then, you won't be allowed in the building.

Bob nods again and takes a short breath. He pushes his chair back, stands, and walks to get his coat from the hook behind his office door. He drapes the coat over his arm, then reaches down to pick up his briefcase, which is standing right below.

—Sorry, Bob. You'll have to leave your briefcase here. Our team needs to go through it. You know, SOP. So, now please vacate your office. Security will escort you to the door.

I turn slightly and beckon with two fingers. Two uniforms come in and flank the inside of the door.

I stand back and let Bob go out first. He turns right and heads down the corridor, a uniform a step behind on either side. I follow.

We let them lead. To give them a sense of dignity, I suppose, so as not to feel like they are being ushered out bodily, like some drunk from a bar. It's funny, but we don't have a good word to describe these people, the ones who've just been fired. "Terminees"? No. They are "former employees" when they are gone, but what do I call Bob today, while he is still in the building? "Rejects" might be closest to the truth, sadly, but it isn't accurate. You reject something at the beginning when you are making your initial choice to hire. Bob was not rejected, he was hired. And kept for a long time.

I wasn't too worried about him, though. After all, there's some decent financial security when this happens. You have your RRSP.

Severance pay is generous enough to justify the non-disclosure agreement. Silence can be remunerative. The company likes to ensure that what happens in Vegas stays in Vegas, so to speak. And similarly, the company gives decent references to former employees. Likes to keep its image as a good place to work shiny.

The corridor is quiet except for the sound of our footfalls. Our pace is—how should I describe it?—purposeful. Bob is leading us as if it were his idea, his project. He hasn't said another word. Some mutter to themselves. Others argue, swear, protest in their office, in the corridor, everywhere. Occasionally one will lose his temper and have to be restrained. But the presence of the uniforms tends to deter that sort of thing. So most are silent like Bob. Keeping their thoughts to themselves.

Basically, my work with Bob himself is already done. What I'm doing now—being part of the exit escort team—is a formality. Maybe having a suit present—not leaving him with just the uniforms—lends a bit of dignity to the process, to the subject. To Bob, that is. For appearances, if nothing else.

A woman walks toward us.

—Hey Bob, how's it goin'?

Then her expression changes. She gets it. Silence.

AS WE MOVE DOWN THE corridor toward the elevators, eyes look away or down, doors close. Mouths about to say something stop, are open and silent for a moment too long then close with as blank an expression as possible. People know what's happening. I can hear the murmurs rise out of the silence as I pass—Bob? Why? What did he do? I always liked him. Such a nice guy. Too bad.

A nice perk of this job is that I get to look at these guys' employment records. Technically I'm just supposed to enter the time and date of termination and schedule the exit interview, then scan whatever paper there is in the file and shred the hard copies. But I take the time to read the files. Call it research. Call it watching my back. I like to find out why the person was fired—if possible. It isn't always.

The yearly performance reviews are there, of course, and they tell part of the story. But all sorts of other tidbits find their way in as well. Suspected—or confirmed—office affairs, insubordination, drugs and drunkenness. A few instances of sexual misconduct. Those are mostly recent. Even mentions of verbal abuse, stuff you used to just have to man up and take. The rules that you have to finesse to stay in the game have changed a bit. You've got to keep current. This I have learned.

The entries in these files are supposed—again, according to the handbook—to be entered only after a formal procedure has been completed. But I don't know, some of it is so petty. Supposed insults and other personal affronts, a surprising number of unprovable, "he said, she said" sort of things, though really most of it is "he said, he said."

So I looked at Bob's file. It was a thick one. Fifty-three, married, three children. Been with the company since he got his MBA, over twenty years ago. His history was pretty average. No black marks. His reviews were by and large good to very good. One of his bosses had called him "predictable," which once might have been a compliment. He plateaued out about five years ago, it looked like. They probably should have let him go then. Those five years could have been useful to another outfit. They're gone now. Can't get them back.

And he got promoted several times. Of course, they promote you so you work to get promoted again. You keep getting promoted until you get fired or become CEO. Or quit when you don't become CEO or whatever was the next target job.

Someone finally decided Bob should go. He'd be given some reasons. There's a whole grab bag of easy justifications—downsizing, low productivity, failure to get along, management change, he didn't fit in with the new team. Whatever. But he probably wouldn't really find out why, not that it made a difference.

Bob seems to have felt secure, doing what he was told to do. Executing his job with his usual efficiency. Did he see it coming? Maybe not. If you are satisfied with your job, or at least comfortable, why would you make the effort to look for another? It might attract attention and itself get you fired.

So what really got Bob fired? Maybe his stats weren't good enough. He was consistent, sure, but after so many years, is being consistent enough? Or do you always have to do more, that little extra to show you still had it, still were hungry? Or maybe he just pissed off someone. Doesn't take much sometimes. You piss off someone with a more expensive suit than yours—you get in their way, you speak too much truth to power, you do your job too well and make them look bad—and you're toast.

I can't see his face, only his back. His footsteps are regular. Is he looking at the floor? No. Some do. And his back is straight, but not overly so. No forced show of pride. No show of defiance, either. He's doing what he always has, getting on by getting along.

I sometimes wonder about people like Bob. Are they really so naïve about life? Do they think they are safe? Life's about competition. You're not protected—not by the company, not by anyone. You compete against others, against the world, all the time. You can't let up. Or that's the end. Game over.

Bob and the uniforms stop in front of the elevator. One of the uniforms pushes the Down button.

The elevator takes a long time to arrive. Bob stares straight at the blank surface of the door the whole time. His shoulders are now a bit stooped, as if tired all of a sudden. The uniforms don't move. Finally the doors open. We all get in. The doors close.

Bob is in the rear. The uniforms and I stay near the front to give him room. The display counts down the floors. It's a big enough elevator, but it always feels small on days like this, like the box it is. With the doors shut and no view out, it seems harder to breathe. Does Bob feel this too? The sense of walls closing in. But he is about to be free of them.

What will he do now? Take time off probably. Regroup. Then try to find another job. Or start his own company, be his own boss. He could become an entrepreneur, or even better, a consultant. Market his experience, his years at the company, to others. All that time has to count for something, doesn't it? There's always opportunity out there. He'll see. He'll energize himself for something. A project, a goal, a passion that the nine-to-five life hasn't allowed him to fully explore. Maybe he already has. So really, maybe we're doing him a favour. Letting him experience life anew. Yeah, that's a good way to look at it.

A tone sounds. The doors open. We move out into the ground-floor corridor. I move to the side. The uniforms wait for Bob to emerge and then take their places behind him again. We walk through the lobby. The receptionist keeps his eyes down, his mouth closed like all the rest.

SOP is to walk the subject to his vehicle and make sure he or she leaves the grounds of the company immediately. I look at my watch. Three-thirty. I still have a shit-load to do today. I tell one of the uniforms to watch and make sure that Bob gets off and doesn't do anything crazy—like crash his car into our boss's on his way out—and I go back to my office.

The afternoon winds down. Some phone calls and e-mails that need to be answered interrupt, but I get done what I need to do today and then arrange what I have to do in the morning. There are a couple of short reports I need to read before leaving, so I open them up and lean back, taking in the details of the proposed campaigns for the marketing of a couple of new products. Late in the afternoon, there is a knock on my office's doorframe.

—Sir?

It's the uniform I left in the parking lot.

—Yes?

—He's off the property, sir. He drove off about—he checks his watch—seven minutes ago.

I look at my watch. It's 5:10.

THE WRITING LIFE

Jerry Levy

MY SHRINK THINKS I SHOULD give up writing. "It's too isolating," he tells me. "Be with people."

Is he kidding? Has he scanned the newspapers lately? Does he know about the hole in the ozone, about the wars and kidnappings and beheadings, about the depletion of natural resources, about the loss of species after species of animals?

Hey, Mr. Psychiatrist! Check out this headline in yesterday's newspaper:

Man Freezes Dead Mother To Collect Benefits.

So, be with people? No thanks, I'll gladly hole myself in my small apartment and write stories instead. Fiction.

But as with everything that has value, there's a price to be paid for pursuing it. I mean, I'm really pretty isolated. Since I started on my novel, what few friends I have I hardly ever see anymore. It would be nice to, I don't know, have a dinner out, see a movie, go for a drive in the country. But my friends are mostly solitary artist types and tend to hibernate, just like me. I suppose I could do these things alone but it seems like too much of an effort.

Then there's my badgering mother. With her cackling, she gets under my skin like no one else: "How do you ever expect to meet someone if you stay home every night writing *silly stories*?"

So I'm forty-two, still unmarried. I know my mother's concerned about me, that I'll end up all alone, an old curmudgeonly bachelor, eating cans of sardines above the sink, food particles nestling in my beard. But silly stories? Really, ma, give me a break. In any case, listen, ma, I don't want to meet someone. Don't you get it? I'm not really suited for anyone, for companionship. And besides, just pick up the newspaper!

Anyway, from time to time I think about forging a different life, maybe getting a real job, the kind that pays decent money. The problem is that I'm not really suited for much. I once worked as a security guard but got fired for writing. Then I worked in a bookstore for a time. You would think that would be a most suitable job for someone like me, and I totally agree. Except for one thing: I have high standards when it comes to reading. So I tried to talk customers out of buying the trashy romance books that they took to the counter.

"You're not serious. I know a much better book for you than the one you want to buy," I would say, going on to explain the virtues of "serious" literature. Ok, so I didn't last long at the bookstore, I think three months. Those damn complaints to the manager did me in. Imagine, I was just trying to educate . . . and I got canned.

So then I tried picking worms at night, but the truth is my eyes aren't good enough for that kind of work—I usually ended up with half a worm in my fingers. Interestingly, I did discover that half a worm can live on quite a long time, squiggly little buggers.

There were other jobs. I cleaned up after the horses at a stable, I washed dishes in a Greek restaurant, I sold lighting fixtures. Anyway, you get it, none of those jobs appealed, none suitable for someone of my calibre.

Anyway, to the point of a real life. Yes, that would be interesting. Not too long ago, I read an article about the great French writer Gustave Flaubert. It seems that one afternoon, as he was passing a playground wherein he spotted a family having fun, he turned to his companion and muttered, *"Ils sont dans le vrai."* What are we to make of such sentiments, that the family was "in the right"? That perhaps real life lies elsewhere, other than in the writer's lair?

So I guess you'd like to know why a seemingly sane man in the prime of life would willingly sit in a chair for hours on end, wracking his brain to come up with, as my mother puts it, silly stories ?

Well, it isn't for the money, I can tell you that. I barely scrape by. I scrounge along on some part-time jobs teaching writing, a few bucks from published stories in magazines, that's about it. At the end of the month, when the rent is to paid, I usually take the back stairs to leave the building. I can't deal with running into the landlord, he of the grubby open palms and scorching eyes that burn holes through me.

"Rent due," is all he says.

He just despises excellence, that's what his problem is. He's all wrapped up with money and banks and cheques and has lost touch with the more aesthetic things in life, things like literature, like my stories.

Let me say this as clear as I can. I don't write as a cry for help, a desire for fame, or because I have something especially important to say; heaven forbid that I should say that I'm enamoured with the process. On the contrary, writing can be pure drudgery. Finding the right sentence to move a story along, agonizingly searching your mind for just the best word to breathe life into a character, endless editing and revisions . . . it's all enough to make you go mad. Oh, and let's not forget all those times when despite your best efforts, the story comes to an impasse and there's nothing more to say, no ideas left to tinker with. You've fallen into a dark chasm of nothingness. "Writer's block," they call it, but I call it pure torture.

Let me tell you what it's really like to devote yourself to writing. First, get used to your own company if you're serious about it. Unplug the phone. Cancel your cable. Close the curtains —if you don't, you'll long to be outside and won't write a word.

And speaking of being outside, don't write in cafés. No real writing takes place there. This isn't 1920's Paris when Hemingway and Sartre and Camus would write in *Les Deux Magots* and *Café de Flore*. If you're trying to write in a café on Bloor Street in Toronto, have a close look at the brunette at the next table—that's not Simone de Beauvoir. And the guy pretending to write in the far corner isn't James Joyce.

As I mentioned, it's a lonely affair, this business of writing. Once when I was at my wit's end and sick of my own company, I called an ad I saw in *Now* magazine. "Are You Looking for a Friend?" it said. So I called. The guy told me he was offering services as a professional friend. "Can you put up with my cynicism?" I asked. "That's what true friends do," I reminded him. "No one understands your genius," he said. "They're jealous of your excellence. That's why you don't have many friends." I was liking him just fine until he told me that he charged $40 to $80 for ahem . . . various assorted jobs. Some friend.

Then there's the whole thing about being poor. Everything in the city entices, and everything is beyond your means. Movies, fine dining, plays. But you make do. You dumpster dive for food and haggle for the clothes prices at Goodwill, which is kind of ridiculous because that money goes to train and shelter the needy.

Anyway, getting back to why I write, it really is a complicated affair. I think I can explain it best by referring to one of my stories in which I tell the tale of a man and his double. Well, the replica looks exactly like the original but is a bit brighter, more suave, certainly more together. As my mother would say, he's a *mensch*. A gentleman.

There you have it—that's why I write, why I have written all these years. It's been in order to create a double. Me and my alter-ego.

And out there in this vast city of Toronto, my double has taken on a life of his own and walks the streets. He's the one who won't be writing because that's much too solitary a craft for him. He's already been through all the therapy he needs. In fact, he's beyond therapy. He's a man in motion. A *bon vivant* of the world.

Restless within the confines of my writer's hole, I'll venture out in the wee hours one night. My head looking up toward the heavens for divine inspiration as I contemplate my next story, not looking where I'm going, I'll bump into him, my more inspired likeness. And then the strangest thing will happen. My body will begin to dissipate quickly, my atoms and molecules starting to merge with his . . . and I, noble writer that I purport to be, will disappear into a greater whole.

THE VETERAN AND THE PASSERBY

Geza Tatrallyay

He was always just standing there, on the corner, down by the parking lot, whenever I went to Safeway. Always tanned, thin but once obviously very fit, with longish hair and piercing blue eyes. On sunny days, in filthy shorts, a torn T-shirt and flip-flops. When colder, in dirty jeans and a tattered Grateful Dead hoodie. A beige, paint-speckled red backpack, presumably holding his meager possessions, placed carelessly against the tree in the corner of the lot. His greasy Giants baseball cap upside down, right there, down on the sidewalk by his always moving feet, a few coins and crumpled dollar bills thrown in, crying out for companions to skip across the void and join them from the pockets of passersby like me.

One of San Francisco's homeless, for sure, I told myself. In unusual territory though—most are down in the Tenderloin area and not in the swanky Marina. Looks like a veteran, too. Iraq, maybe? Or Afghanistan?

Who is this fucker anyway? This weird guy who always looks me over, this pervert who stares at me as he goes by? First, with his nerdish rucksack, all floppy and empty, slung on one shoulder. Thinks he is so fucking nonchalant, the asshole does. Then, eons later, on his way back, filled to the brim, so that the motherfucker looks like he's struggling to carry the weight of the world on his shoulders. Like Jesus Christ carrying the fucking cross on his way to Golgotha or something. Shit, this guy would've never made it over in the Sandpit, that's a given, wearing battle rattle and all—the weight alone would have killed the sucker in a sec. The Hajis would have downed him for sure, first time out.

Jake—for that is what he told me he was called, when after passing him I finally asked him his name when he grunted a thanks for the dollar bill I dropped into the cap—was always chatting away, mumbling something *sotto voce* to himself. Who knows about what and why, but I heard the low muttering often enough on my trips to the grocery store, so that one Friday morning when Marcia was looking after the grandkids and I had nothing pressing on my agenda, on the spur of the moment, I decided, why not talk to the guy, see what he has to say for himself. So I invited Jake for a coffee at Starbucks just up the street. He was rather taken aback by the invitation, but seemed okay with it, maybe a bit torn at first though, since he would have to relinquish his usual spot for a while.

And now the a-hole is saying something to me—what the fuck? He's asking me if I want to go to Starbucks with him. Says he'll buy me a coffee. Is he making a pass at me, the queer geezer? Well, maybe no harm, I can certainly handle the fucker if he tries to suck me off. At least I will get a cup of joe and a muffin out of it. Haa!

I ordered a large coffee with milk and lots of sugar and a blueberry muffin for Jake, a cappuccino for myself. We sat down at a corner table, putting our twin backpacks at our feet. He held his paper cup with both hands, slowly slurping the hot liquid through the lid, occasionally glancing up at me.

"Thanks, man," he finally blurted out, breaking the silence between us. I sensed real gratitude there—it seemed, from the way he looked at me, that this was the first time in a while anyone had invited him for a coffee. Or, for anything.

"No problem, Jake," I answered, pleased. Then after a pause, while our eyes met, "Where are you from?"

Jesus, he just won't let up with the questions will he, the fucker? I have already told him my name—not my real one, of course—and now he wants to know where I'm from. Christ, what the fuck for? Jesus, this is like being questioned by fucking al Qaeda—you know, name rank and serial number—just before they beat the holy living shit outta you.

Of course, Jake gave me an inane answer—that now he was just from here. I left it at that and rather asked him as nonchalantly as I could, "So, I am intrigued, Jake—why do you stand on that corner down by Safeway every day?"

So now the cocksucker, he wants to know why I stand where I stand whenever I want to. Well, fuck nuts, isn't it obvious? Because it's a good place to watch dick fingers like you march past and stare at me. And, just maybe, to collect a few coins.

Jake looked at me as if I was plain stupid, without deigning to give me an answer.

I let silence rule while he munched on his muffin. "So Jake"—I wanted to probe what happened to the guy, but by this time, I was ready to believe that this too might be futile—"where were you stationed? Will you tell me what happened over there? May I ask, Jake—do you have PTSD?"

There, I finally got the question out, the one I had been wanting to ask my coffee companion all along.

Fuck, man! The dude now wants to know what happened—what the fuck for? Whether I have PTSD—of course, you asshole, can't you see? Can't you fucking TELL?

I could see that this set of questions did not sit well, because Jake took a big gulp of his coffee and then just sat there, eyes vacant, looking into his cup, not saying anything. But I thought there was something going on in that mind of his, though I wasn't entirely sure.

Okay, you jerkoff, Stan—or whatever the fuck you said your name was. I'll tell you, what happened. Of course, you and all the other little pricks and cunts we went over there for will never really know what it was like when we were out in the red zone. Whatever I might be able to tell you here in fucking Cow Hollow will pale to what the reality actually was.

Jake's mien had suddenly taken on an angry character, almost vicious.

And never mind, all the killing and maiming that went on before the straw that broke the camel's back (motherfucker, excuse the sick sandy pun)—the semblance of a smile had appeared on his face—*you sort of get inured to it all after a while. Although, progressively, the horror of it builds up, weighs on you—not you, asshole, because you never went. But we were fucking there to do a job. We were there to kill or be killed.*

I could see that Jake's lips were moving—or perhaps trembling—but nothing audible came out from them. He just kept staring ahead without looking at anything.

Okay, jerkoff, what finally did me in, happened three weeks before the end of my second tour. My two best buddies and I—we were out looking for IEDs—asshole, that's short for improvised explosive devices—because the fucking Hajis would stick them all over so that we would knock against them or step on them. They just tried to shove them up our collective ass, they did, wherever we were. Finding them was laborious work, and you had to sort of do it by feel. And unless you sensed one, smelled it or used fucking ESP to ferret it out, you were likely to be blown to smithereens.

So my two mates, Bob and Will, were doing this excruciating job, while I was a few paces behind monitoring three sixty for the fucking Muj. Yeah, the shit asses would come out of nowhere and fucking do a death blossom that was sure to blow your head off if you were in the way. Will, who had just started his first tour in the Sandbox and didn't have a shitload of experience, fucking poked the sand with his HK G3—and BAMM! A bloody mega-explosion right in front of me. I hit the dirt, went under, unconscious.

Jake's hands suddenly flew up in the air and from his eyes I could now see that he was getting worked up, but still no sound emanated from his mouth.

"Jake, it's all right," I said, as I looked around, not wanting him to make a scene. "You don't need to tell me if you don't want to."

Fuck, man! Just shut up and listen. I don't know how long I was out, but it couldn't have been more than a few minutes, because a wildfire was still raging right in front of me. I had gone stone deaf, could not hear a fucking thing. I slowly pulled myself together, a few bruises here and there, my left arm lacerated, bleeding badly.

I ripped off what was left of my battle rattle, got down to my undershirt, which I just tore off my shaking body and used it to bandage what was fucking left of my arm.
Then I looked around.

Across the table from me, Jake seemed to be favouring his left arm, holding it with his right hand. He swivelled his head as if to check out the neighbouring tables—maybe he thought he was making a spectacle of himself. Then his eyes went to the floor as if he had dropped something. His face contorted in a terrified grimace.

My buddies were nowhere. I looked again, down low. Strewn around all over the fucking desert were body parts. A bleeding hand still twitching, a boot with part of a calf protruding, tendons and bloody flesh and all, half of what may have been Will's head, just flesh, brains, hair and blood all over, including, as I looked again at myself, on me. I blinked, hoping the horror scene would go away—and puked my insides out, right there in the fucking sand. When I got up from my knees, I was shaking and bawling like I hadn't since I was a babe—for fuck's sake, Will was just a child—he still carried around a picture of his mom—and Bob, he was the joker in the crew, a fucking strongman.

I looked at him puzzled, as I could see tears well in his eyes, one dropping on the lid of his cup.

Here one second, pulp the next.
From dust to dust. The only thing fucking religion ever got right, I tell you.
When I had no more tears to shed, I realized there was nothing I could do for my buddies, so I did another three sixty scan, looked around in the sand to see if any of our weapons were still intact,

and seeing this was hopeless, started hightailing it back toward where I thought the FOB was—the Forward Operating Base, you asshole. In retrospect, I know some would say I was goddam lucky, because within what seemed like only moments, a gun truck pulled up and two of our grunts jumped out and fucking hoisted me in, lock stock and barrel. I vaguely remember them telling me before I passed out they had heard the blast and got there as soon as they could.

Jake wiped his eyes with his sleeves before taking another sip of his coffee.

I came to, sometime later back at the FOB on a hospital cot. Noticed my arm was all bandaged up. Doctor came over in a little while, told me my arm would be okay, asked me a few questions—my hearing was still not a hundred per cent—but I knew he was fucking assessing me. He told me I would be sent home on the next transport.

I was angry, because, fuck, I just wanted to get out there again and shoot up as many Haji as I could before I went home. To avenge Will and Bob. And all the others. When the doctor left, I got out of bed, and tried to get out of the fucking hospital to get my hands on any kind of a submachine gun or grenade launcher, even though my fucking arm would have made it difficult to operate one of these. Two cock-sucking male nurses grabbed me, though, took me back to bed, and said I had better stay put or they would have to put me in the cage.

The next day they let me go back to the barracks to await transfer back home the following week. But sure as hell, I was not going to fucking lie on my cot and just beat off all day. There were enough arms around in the room, some of my buddies' automatics, so . . .

All of a sudden Jake jumped up from his seat and started making like he was shooting an imaginary automatic gun. I grabbed him by the elbow, scooped up the two backpacks with the other hand, and led him out onto the sidewalk.

"Jake, my friend, are you all right?" I asked, shaking him by the shoulders.

It took him a moment or two to recover and pull himself out of what must have been some kind of a trance, reliving some horrific experience.

Then with a grimace, looking at me, he slowly answered, "Yes, Stan."

"Are you sure? What was going on there?"

Fuck. Not again. The dude wants to know what I . . . Never fucking mind.

Then Jake said, "Thanks for the coffee. See you around, Stan. Down by Safeway. Maybe."

I watched him shuffle slowly down the hill in his flip-flops, shaking his head and muttering something.

THE NEXT MORNING, A SATURDAY, Marcia and I were having a late breakfast after a night out on the town, and just as I was taking our soft-boiled eggs out of the boiling water, a deafening blast shook the whole building. It penetrated my whole being so I knew it couldn't have come from very far away. We looked at each other, I uttered the words, "What the . . . ?" then we hurried outside up to a spot where I could get a better view. Our attention went immediately over to where there was a huge pillar of black smoke rising high in the sky and where all the sirens seemed to be focusing. About a mile away, I guessed. And then it hit me: that was where Safeway was.

"Let's get over there," I said to Marcia. "I want to go see what happened." Of course, I was a bit concerned for my coffee mate.

Marcia was a little dubious, although I was the one who usually tried to avoid potential hotspots, but she came along.

When we got near, we saw that the police had already cordoned the site off. Where the Safeway had been, was now a gaping hole, with flames still leaping up here and there from what remained of our local grocery store.

I looked around to see if Jake was in his usual spot, but that corner too, had been blown away, and was well within the cordoned area.

"Excuse me, sir," I addressed one of the policemen who were teeming around the area, "can you tell us what happened?"

"Well, it seems a bomb was detonated at Safeway less than an hour ago."

"Any idea of who did it? And why?"

"Nope," the officer responded. "I doubt we'll ever know for sure."

BACK HOME, WE TURNED ON the local news. ". . . officials are still not sure of the death toll in the tragic bombing at Safeway today. At least a hundred people might have been there on such a fine Saturday morning, a Safeway spokeswoman told us. It will take some time for authorities to get a handle on the number of casualties. And police still have no idea of what caused the blast—forensic experts are combing over the site. Was it an accident? An act of terrorism? If so, who did it, and why? These are the questions the authorities hope to find answers to over the next several days."

THE DAYS PASSED, AND OFFICIALDOM concluded, based on some forensic evidence, that it likely was a bombing, some kind of homemade bomb—what soldiers call an improvised explosive device, an IED.

Each morning, I wandered over to as close to the spot where Jake used to hang out as I could, and walked from there up to Starbucks for my coffee, then back down again to the bombing site. But I never saw my friend again.

I even made some discreet enquiries in local hospitals, but a wiry veteran called Jake had not registered anywhere.

He must have perished in the bombing, I lamented to myself. And, when I thought about our coffee at Starbuck's the day before the explosion, in my heart of hearts, I was sure that Jake was the tortured being who had planted and detonated the IED.

A homeless veteran, who, along with his buddies, had given all for his country, which in the end, was just not there for him.

So he took his revenge the only way he knew how. And to boot, it also ended the searing pain of his memories.

A *win-win*.

THE MAN WHO DREAMED OF BEING NOAH

Jerry Levy

H<small>E WASN'T MUCH</small>—at least that's what people always thought. In grade school, he sat at the very back of the classroom, praying the teachers wouldn't call on him. And they never did. They somehow knew to leave David Schmulich alone. And it was the same throughout high school. He was a non-entity in the world of academia, barely squeaking by. In fact, the only attention he ever received was from a gang of high school bullies, who gave him a wedgie and stuck him on a fence post (he was rescued by a teacher).

Things improved a bit once he left school. He took the only job he could find, working as a clerk in a hardware store. It wasn't a bad fit—David liked nuts and bolts; he really preferred cold steel and aluminum and the world of small gadgets to people. He worked five days a week and every second Saturday. As for his personal life, he married the first woman he ever dated; Bernice

Rothman had walked into the hardware store and asked about stripping for the crack in her door, to keep out the cold draft. Then she asked about mouse traps because she had seen a few of the furry rodents in her house. Then about caulking for her bathroom ceiling because some water had leaked through the roof. She enquired about how to reattach siding because strong gusts of wind had caused a couple of pieces to hang precariously . . . she even showed David a picture of the damage on her phone. In all, she was at the store for close to two hours and David fell madly in love. It didn't matter that Bernice was terribly overweight or had pockmarked skin, he felt helpful to someone for once in his life and so asked her out. Their first date was to an ice cream parlour and they gorged on desserts—David ordered a Belgium waffle with sliced banana, Nutella and French pralines, topped with a dollop of chocolate ice cream. Bernice ordered a waffle cone with mint ice cream, fresh strawberries, and French dark chocolate sauce. Aside from his mother, it was the first time in David's life that he felt comfortable enough in front of a woman that he could actually eat a meal and so soon after that date, some two weeks later, in fact, David decided to propose.

DAVID MOVED FROM HIS PARENT'S small apartment into Bernice's house. The siding that was hanging wasn't high up so he climbed a ladder and tacked it back into place. He set mouse traps and even caught three of the vermin. He fixed the bathroom ceiling, using an Exacto knife to cut out the affected water-damaged area and then priming the area with sandpaper and plaster; finally, he painted. David was a tinkerer. He was particularly good with his hands, and Bernice took pride in his abilities.

As for her part, Bernice worked as a waitress in a diner. It was an okay job, she didn't mind it, and because she was so friendly with customers, she made good money on tips. Still, at the end of each day, her feet hurt, and David massaged them. She knew it wasn't the type of work she wanted to do the rest of her life and harboured a dream of opening her own café. She could bake, oh how she could bake—apple pies and spice cakes and scones being her forte.

So, one day, when she approached David about the possibility of opening a café, a small one that would serve coffee and desserts and maybe salads for lunch, he thought it a marvellous idea. So too, did her parents, who would help her with the initial financing (they also helped her buy her house). And that was how Beanie's Café was born.

ALTHOUGH BERNICE GAVE UP HER waitressing job, David kept his own job; the pair needed the security of his full-time income. But he helped around Beanie's whenever he could, fixing things, and cleaning. Usually, this all took place after he left his hardware job for the day, around five o'clock. He loved being an entrepreneur; it made him feel much more accomplished than normal. And of course, he was incredibly happy for Bernice, the woman he loved.

Still, something rankled in David. It usually came about when he would mop up Beanie's at the end of the day. The café would close, Bernice would leave, and David would stand with mop in hand. The café was stock-still. A thought bubbled into his brain at those times, and it was this: *I might be more than I seem. I can be more than I seem.*

So an idea was hatched in David's brain, a far-fetched idea that he kept to himself. He didn't even tell his wife. But the idea gave way to a certain alter-reality and it made him put aside the mop and listen intently. He heard them, he really did. Or at least, he believed he heard them—they manifested for David Schmulich—and that was enough for him. But they were so strange, these high-pitched sounds. The only time he had ever heard anything like it was when he saw a National Geographic documentary on orca whales that had separated from their pod.

The longer he listened, the more confused he became as to exactly where they were emanated. He checked the men's and women's bathrooms on the floor below but there was no one there. The boiler room equipment hummed as usual. He peered into the oven, the freezer, the fridge: everything was operating normally.

David stood in the middle of the café, resting his chin and hands on the end of the mop. It had been a month and three days since he and his wife opened Beanie's Café. And life was good. Maybe now it would become even better, at least for him. For David Schmulich, who had been ignored his entire life. Who had been a non-entity from the day he was born. Now things would change, and David knew exactly how.

That night, David mentioned to Bernice the strange sounds he had heard.

"Maybe there's an animal living somewhere in the roof," she offered. "We should get someone to check it out. If it's a squirrel or raccoon or even a family of pigeons, we have to get them out before they cause any real damage."

David knew it was no animal in the roof that he heard. Still, it was a perfect start, exactly what he needed, and so he agreed he would call an animal control company in the morning.

"Interesting job?" asked David, standing next to the aluminum ladder that the pest control technician was climbing. He had taken the day off work to deal with the technician.

"Not bad. I've seen some interesting things. Rattlers that have gotten loose in houses, alligators that have outgrown bathtubs, Once caught a baby Bengal tiger. Usually, it's wild animals that people keep as pets that cause trouble."

"Well, I don't think there's a tiger in the roof," chuckled David.

"No," shouted the technician, now firmly perched on top of the roof, "but you might have something living in the crawlspace between the roof and the joists. Probably best to remove a few shingles to make sure."

"How much is this going to cost?" called out David, his hands cupped around his mouth for greater amplification.

"It's conditional."

"On what?"

"On the conditions we find. You can't really anticipate all the possible conditions."

It turned out there were no conditions, no animals living at the top of Beanie's. Nor at the bottom. Of course, David already knew that. But the cost for the pest technician and the roofer amounted close to seven hundred dollars. A princely sum, but it was all a means to an end, so David didn't mind.

After the technician left, David helped out in the café—he made turkey and ham and cheese wraps. And at the end of the day, after the din of noise coming from the busy café—patrons talking in loud voices, the espresso machine hissing, waves of music—he was happy for the silence.

So in the evening, long after the café had closed and his wife gone, David made himself a coffee and munched on an oatmeal cookie. He rolled his head around and around, trying to work out the kinks. It had been a long, expensive day. He took a deep breath and closed his tired eyes.

All is peace, he thought. All is peace, he repeated to himself. It was a mantra he had picked up in a relaxation class he took during his high school days after he had been bullied and hung on a fence post to wither. He imagined warm sand squishing up between his toes. A walk in the spongy, idyllic side of life. David gave his head a shake and picked up the mop. Best to get on with things. He was truly eager to leave this day behind him and he swept the floor hurriedly in great big arcs.

When the landline phone in the house rang at exactly 3:12 a.m., David was in his lobster boat, hauling up a trap. Stuffed lobster tails, lobster pie. Shrimp and scallops. A bottle of white wine. His mouth watered as he thought about dinner. Waves slapped the boat as David examined his catch.

Bernice pushed at his ragged shoulders as the phone rang on insistently.

"Pick it up," she implored.

Roused from his reverie, David didn't know where he was. He raised a hand to pull up the next lobster trap but instead picked up the phone.

"Bring up the haul," he uttered dreamily.

"What?"

"Hello?" said David tentatively, now semi-awake.

"David, you've got a problem."

"Who is this?" asked David, sitting up in bed.

"Wilbur Roberts."

David knew Wilbur as the head veterinarian and owner of the animal clinic adjacent to Beanie's.

It was freezing cold when David stepped out into the night, still wearing his pyjamas and slippers. He ran the four blocks to the café where he met up with Wilbur. Unlocking the front door, the two men were greeted with three feet of water

"My assistant was up babysitting a sick German Shepherd when she heard a couple of big bangs. Sounded like a shotgun, she said. So she called me."

His body shuddered as David waded through the quagmire. Water was up to his knees as cups and saucers floated by. "Must be a broken pipe," he shouted.

In fact, it was two broken pipes. Both having burst in the exact spots David had cut them earlier that day. When the plumber came, he quickly shut off the water and showed David the damage.

"Not sure how it happened," he said, puzzled. "Usually when pipes give way it's because they're corroded. But these pipes were in perfect condition. The other thing is that they were so far removed from each other. I mean, one of the broken pipes is just under the sink and the other in the washroom. They're not related. If I didn't know better, I'd say this was a case of vandalism."

Vandalism? thought David. Good guess.

Beanie's was closed for the next two days. The broken pipes were replaced and dehumidifiers and fans installed to remove excess moisture. Total cost: twenty-eight hundred fifty-five dollars. Not including two days of lost revenue.

"No need to be concerned," David told Bernice confidently. "We'll make it up. Don't worry, it'll all work out in the end."

But Bernice was concerned. It seemed they had run into a spate of bad luck. Strange sounds, now broken water pipes. Uncanny bad luck.

FOR THE NEXT TWO WEEKS, business at the café returned to normal. David and Bernice forgot about the two bizarre episodes. But as David was cleaning up one night he heard the sounds again. Yes, he was sure he heard them. Two weeks was long enough. He put down the broom and stopped to listen. This time they were considerably louder. Spilling forth from the walls and floors. Every surface in the café seemed to be vibrating with sound. Despite that and as odd as it seemed, David again couldn't tell where they originated. It was a diffused sound and growing, tracing a route throughout the café. David held his hands over his ears and gritted his teeth like he was suffering from a drug-induced hallucination. "Enough already," he said to himself. "I get it."

Desperate, he called his wife.

"Please come," he urged.

When Bernice arrived, David said in fright: "This place doesn't accept us." Although his wife was not one to give in to such frivolous metaphysical talk, she didn't discount what David had said. Something indeed was amiss.

"I don't hear anything," she said.

"Well, I did. It seems to have stopped now. But it was like listening to someone wailing from the bottom of a well when you're standing at the top. It was so distant that it was almost not here."

He needed something more of course. And so he continued on. It was a gamble, a big one, but he knew Bernice believed in him.

"And I saw something," he said. "I know it sounds crazy but I saw a ghost. Well, actually a couple of them. The ghosts appeared fragmented, not quite fully developed, and yet, I could make out their outlines. They were all wearing moccasins and had fabric leggings. The men wore felt hats with feathers sticking out, and they carried rifles. The women petticoats with aprons and white caps. But they didn't last long, they disappeared."

Bernice looked askance at David, walked to the front door, and left without saying another word.

The next day, while Bernice tended to the café, David again took a day off work and this time, went to the library. With great attention to detail, he rifled through page after page of city archives, trying to find out the history of Toronto, especially the area around Beanie's.

What he uncovered was a Pandora's Box of solid history that he could use to his advantage. It seemed that very close to Beanie's, a half block away, in fact, the area had been a burial site! A very small graveyard going back to 1793. With his jaw slack, like it had become unhinged, David read in the city archives that the land had once been a resting place for early settlers. Pioneers. For reasons that were not clearly spelled out, the burial land was paved over, leading the way for commercial use.

When David returned to the café, the eight small, wall-mounted speakers were playing Tony Bennett's 'I Left My Heart in San Francisco.'

"Appropriate song," said David to Bernice. "'Cause something got left here in this very space . . . right in the ground. Right below."

He went on to explain to her what he had found. A wave of nausea overtook Bernice and she had to sit down.

"The burial site, right below Beanie's. It's hard to believe. What are we going to do?" she mused in a low voice.

It was true, he had fudged the truth a bit. To suit his needs . . . a half block away, a block away, it really didn't matter.

"Make things right," answered David confidently.

DAVID DUG HIS HEEL INTO the soft earth and looked out at the still lake. He had never been here before and came in spite of Bernice's objections. "The early settlers lived and worked off the land," he had told her. "Maybe I can find what we need at the lake."

"I don't know what's gotten into you," Bernice had replied. "It's preposterous. If you cared, you'd know I need you here at the café, not foraging about looking for God-knows-what in the forest."

But David feared that the strange sounds and ghost-like figures might eventually turn up during business hours and drive customers away—in fact, he would see to it. He was in the forest precisely because he cared. Cared about his own agenda.

He sat down on the exposed roots of a huge oak tree and snapped a fallen twig in half. If nothing else, it was certainly peaceful here, a watercolour sketch of nature. The lake was smooth, the air light and fragrant, the earth soft and warm. David was enveloped in a deep silence that was broken only by the sweet song of birds. He reached down and grabbed a handful of dark earth, rolling it in his hand.

A chipmunk stood on its hind legs to look at David and then skittered away under a log. David got onto his hands and knees and looked under it. His ear precipitously close to the ground, he heard things. There were the birds, of course, but now he could hear the other sounds of the forest, the murmuring of the water nearby, the whistling of the wind through the treetops, the chirping of insects, the tapping of a woodpecker against a tree trunk. A secret world that beat to its own unique rhythm.

David continued to listen for a long while, intoxicated by the beauty of forest life. At last, he stood up, buoyed by an epiphany of sorts. Perhaps what he was supposed to find lay right before him, that nature itself, with its bountiful harmony, was the answer. It was the answer. One he had been looking for all his life.

He walked along a path adjacent to the shoreline and came to a beaver's dam. He took a deep breath and watched hypnotized as a family of beavers swam below the surface of the water, next to the dam. They surfaced and clambered onto the wood, shaking water from their slick fur. Rows of branched entanglements radiated life and the dam became dense with activity. Nature without limits, immortal.

He would have stayed in this place even longer, broadening his understanding, but knew he had work to do back in the café.

David returned to Beanie's and told Bernice about his visit to the lake. "I think I know what has to be done," he told her. "I mean, it's not like I know for sure. I could be totally off-base. It's only kind of a hunch actually. Intuition. But I feel it's what the pioneers would want."

David took a deep breath and continued on. "It's hard to articulate in any way that makes sense and maybe it doesn't make any sense at all. I guess you'll have to trust me because I have to act on it."

"I have no one else to trust," said Bernice, dumbfounded. "I love you."

Over the next few days, David took time off work and made a daily visit to the lake, where he collected into a cloth bag fallen tree branches, twigs, rocks, pine cones, leaves, earth. And each day he returned to the café and deposited his findings into a corner of the kitchen. When he determined that he had enough material, he set out late one evening to begin the construction.

He used water to moisten the earth and thin rope to adhere to things. He worked effortlessly, feeling his way along, unafraid to make mistakes. It turned out there were, in fact, no mistakes—things moulded into shape and stuck together. It was an easy construction as if someone were guiding David's hands. The end product was beautifully formed, as in an elegant dream of serenity and wisdom.

He called his wife to view the finished project. It was nearly three a.m. by the time Bernice made it to Beanie's. "Have you gone mad?" she exclaimed. "You built this . . . this thing right in the very centre of the café! What will people say when they see a beaver dam? They'll walk right back out the door, that's what they'll do! Why didn't you put it out of sight, way in the back? Or better yet, why didn't you just call in an exorcist to get rid of the spirits?"

"It belongs here," was all David would say. "In the middle. Don't ask me how I know. I just do. Putting it anywhere else wouldn't be right."

So it was that Beanie's café ended up with a beaver dam. It was no bother at all to patrons, who thought the installation a clever art project. Everyone stopped to run their hands along the construction. Some put flowers between the branches. Others Canadian flags. It was sturdy enough that children sat on top. The dam drew considerable interest after it was talked about in newspaper articles. Words like unique, unusual, surreal, extraordinary, permeated the reports. David's favourite was the following: "The dam in Beanie's seems inexplicably linked to something essential, in which words simply do not suffice, Rather, it must be experienced." David liked that one a lot. He realized that the journalist was right—words really didn't matter. What did was that all the strange sounds stopped. No pipes broke. David knew that neither would ever surface again. Especially now that he had exacted his revenge. Revenge against all who had ignored him his entire life . . . he was now a somebody.

One night, as David and Bernice sat on top of the dam, sipping languidly on coffees and looking out at the moonlight, the earth beneath them began to shake. Then the voices started up once again, louder than ever.

"Hear that? The voices?" said David.

"No."

"I do," said David. "Let's go."

That was it. David and Bernice slid down the dam, locked the door to the café, and hightailed it back to their house where they hid under covers in bed.

"Right in the middle, huh?" whispered Bernice. "And all these sounds that you can hear but I can't. Ha!" With that, she turned her back to David and went to sleep.

There's only one thing left to do, thought David. And it was not long before he, too, dove into the sanctity of deep sleep.

In the early morning, while Bernice was still asleep, David went back to the lake and collected two turtles, big fat spotted ones, which he brought back to the café. It was an easy transition for the creatures—the dam at Beanie's was nice and moist and there were plenty of places to burrow into, branches to climb over. David made sure they had plenty of foliage to eat, and even went to a pet store to stock up on turtle food.

Of course, the children who visited the café thought the turtles totally amazing. They had never seen wild turtles before, and certainly none in a coffee shop. They even named them—Tutu and Mudpie.

But Bernice wasn't too thrilled. She thought David was losing his mind, especially after he told her what was next.

"I think we really need to make a splash with the ghosts and give them a full-blown taste of nature. They really loved the outdoors, had lived all their lives off the land. With animals."

"What are you planning?" said Bernice, tapping the side of her head with her forefinger.

"Don't give me that. I'm not crazy."

But when David said that he planned to capture a couple of frogs and bring them to Beanie's, she knew that he was, in fact, losing it. The problem was that short of divorcing him, which she didn't really want to do since she loved David with all her heart, she really didn't know what to do. Still, she stood up for herself:

"If you bring them in, that'll be the end of us."

"No, it won't. You're my wife and you have to stick by me."

"Like hell I do."

It was the first time in their married life that they had come close to an argument.

But the conversation didn't deter David. Knowing the frogs needed a body of water to frolic in, he brought in an engineer to design a moat around the dam. It wasn't cheap, but David knew that money no longer mattered—what did was quelling the spirits. Quelling his inner spirits, that is.

Catching the two frogs was the easy part and once they were safely ensconced within their new home, David stood back to admire his handiwork.

Some patrons, however, were not so pleased. With frogs and turtles within a dam surrounded by a moat, they called the Department of Health, who quickly shut down Beanie's and gave David thirty days to get rid of the dam and all the animals.

As for Bernice, once David told her what was next, she packed her bags and left.

"Call me once you've come to your senses," she said.

"You're worse than the man from the Department of Health," said David.

His wife leaving was a mere trifle to him. He loved her dearly but he had work to do. His life's work. And with the café closed, it was easier for him to go about doing it. Especially now that he kept the blinds drawn. He took a leave of absence from his hardware job so he had all the time in the world.

Every day, totally unencumbered, he made a trip to the lake and brought back a variety of animals and insects and bugs which he captured in cloth bags or sometimes in simple plastic containers . . . two of each, until the café was quite overrun by the menagerie. There were squirrels and beavers and water skidders and frogs and worms and crows and owls and rabbits and foxes and so many others, that it was only kept manageable because David wrote down everything on his laptop. So that he always knew what was coming in and what he had. Of course, he couldn't capture some of the larger animals himself, like the beavers and foxes, so he enlisted the aid of a wildlife company to help him. They were decent, those guys. "It's for an art installation," David told them. "They'll all be in cages in the café, and they're all going right back to the forest once it's over. Just for a day or two."

If there was a problem, it was that he needed more land in the café. The one mound, the dam, was getting far too crowded. So he constructed many more mounds adjacent to the original dam.

Some of the creepy-crawlies and animals and birds were natural enemies, that was a bigger problem. So to solve that, he kept some in cages, while others he let roam freely. It wasn't the best solution, David knew because the animals in cages missed their freedom. But for the moment, and until he came up with a better idea, it would have to do.

The creatures that seemed to run amok were the snakes. The two of them, whom David named Pamuk and Orkestra, bit everything in sight . . . friend and foe alike. They just couldn't control themselves. So David picked them up with a very long pair of silver tongs and whipped them out the front door onto the sidewalk.

"Banished!" he cried.

As if that weren't bad enough, yet another issue that arose is that the moat couldn't house all the wildlife; he really needed more water. So he used a hose to water down Beanie's until the entire café was literally flooded, save for the mounds of earth where the rabbits and other land animals made their homes. A very expensive espresso machine floated by and was quickly seized upon by a pair of ducks, who tried in vain to make a nest atop it. They had better luck with a toaster since it was quite flat on its side.

So Beanie's turned into one very large snarling, hissing, spitting, growling, yapping, cawing, chirping, coffee house. It wasn't easy for David for he had no one to rely on. So he took to drinking large quantities of liquor and pretty soon let his appearance go. His beard grew long and white and the liquor bulged out his stomach so that he looked quite portly.

Naturally, Wilbur next door was none too pleased. He threatened David and shook his fist at him, but David explained, in a sober moment, that it was all for a greater cause, that one day, any misery experienced by Wilbur would pass, and things would return to normal.

And so it did. Endowed with a certain eternity, it was as if Beanie's now housed a presence that kept the harmony, maintaining the voices of things past. Voices from David's own past. For not a peep further was heard from the spirits. Above the din of the animal noises, David listened intently for them. Nothing. Absolutely nothing. The only sound out of the ordinary was the creaking noises as the café was shifting off the building's foundations. And if he didn't know better, David could have sworn, a squirrel sitting on one shoulder, a chipmunk on the other, that the entirety of Beanie's was slowly drifting away.

LYCANTHROPY

Michael Mirolla

MEN FROM THE OTHER VILLAGES have joined us. And we're searching for him now, each one of us with a grim tattoo on his face, beating methodically the bushes and shrubs on the surrounding hillsides. With sharp sticks, later to be used as tomato-plant stakes and faggots. Already, we've flushed several quivering rabbits and a mother quail. Which immediately gave us the broken-wing signal. "Be careful with the nest," the blacksmith mutters, wiping his eyes with charcoaled hands. The creatures dart away, then turn to stare wide-eyed, surprised that we ignore them. For we've been known to tear a rabbit limb from limb while its heart still beats, to stuff fur and all into our maws. No one's hungry. We'll mark the spot and return another day for any unfinished business.

[Last night, in the middle of the silver-dazzled night, the moon set to slice the mountain tops, he crawled through an open window. Plopped softly to the floor. Nipped with canine teeth the breast of the blacksmith's daughter. There must have been a scream. But no one heard it. She simply didn't arise this morning for breakfast. He howled as the moon drew his throat. I was too sleepy to recognize what he was saying. That he had nipped the breast of the blacksmith's daughter. That she had jerked up with her hand on the mutilated breast, a splotch of red against fervent white. Looked with dumb terror and slowly-stretching mouth at his head. At his smiling, tilting, quizzical head. That she had for a moment gazed past him to a gathering of surrogate stars (for she'd only imagined their existence). That she had fallen back. That the thick moonlight was, at last, penetrating her face. My wife shivered, rose from the bed and squatted in the corner, the steam rising warm beneath her. Shivering, she slipped beneath the quilt, cupped herself against the hollows of my body. We made signs of the cross, offered a prayer to the Virgin and returned to our separate dreams.]

The women in the village, after dressing her in donated white, have begun to pile wood in the central square. Each family provides a portion of the ritual cord necessary to do the job. Some give a little less as they are old and beyond most harm. Others donate more. They have daughters the same age. Or sons that might begin to howl. Still, others chain their horses to huge logs resembling desiccated monsters and drag them groaning to the square. These dig their limbs into the ground and resist. To no avail. For many days, till the cleansing rain, these grooves will be the only reminders of what has taken place—like the slashes of a desperate giant. We'll all be careful not to step in them. She might begin to bleed again.

[Truth is. We had thought little of him till he stole her nipple. He lived alone in the mountains. In the high caves, adapting to his four-legged existence with the ease of someone who had planned it all in advance. But he disturbed no one, and his occasional howls blended in with those of the real wolves. I, of course, recognized the difference. When I wanted to.

Still, we have no quarrel with the fiend. We all know what it means to fall beneath his shadow. We all know. Daily, we are flooded with stories of his new conquests. Of those we thought incorruptible succumbing to his blandishments, falling away like withered branches from the great tree. And daily, the army of misshapen animals he has gathered to worship at his altar grows. Strengthens. Gains momentum. Yet, as you can see, we are understanding folk. Unlike other villages that rounded them all up on the occasion of the first full moon when they emerged and went in search of plateaus. We let him be. "Let him be," the blacksmith said at the time. "Even my hammer does bad work once in a while." It was to his daughter he'd once been engaged. Was all set to marry.]

We're only beating these bushes as a token measure. I know where he is. And I'll lead them there when the time comes. For the moment, unsure as we might be of everything else—this is our first hunt—it's certain that the capture must be effected at night. So we have spent the afternoon moving in the wrong direction. Towards the village. Sometimes beating the same area two and three times. Overturning boulders where only mice and millipedes could hide. Some of our more impetuous youths, so filled with the noonday lust of life, insist we haul him in immediately and "make an example of him." They know none of the rituals. (It must be admitted that even the most experienced among us are only vaguely aware of them). But there is one fundamental fact: it must be done after the sun goes down. Else, she won't revive. They ask why. I don't explain. They mumble words under their breaths and mutter accusations of false compassion. Because he's part of my family. Because he's my older brother. But I don't have to answer them. If they're not careful, they'll return less an eye. Or holding a useless arm. In such a case, I'm perfectly within my rights to defend my name. Even the blacksmith himself, beating the bushes with the same steady hand he uses drumming on Easter Sunday, doesn't insist.

[The circuses, the former leper colonies, the prisons, are packed to the brim with people who can't stop dancing. Or howling. Or flicking their tongues. And even though it's against some law, their keepers are provided with a steady supply of tarantulas. A sting for a dance. They recruit them from the hills. String them in long untethered lines (for who among them would dream of escape?). Dancers, wolves, spiders, songbirds, bees, snakes. But we in the village are enlightened. Have no use for such nonsense. And cruelty. Besides, Our Holy Mother Church has proven they're highly infectious. That they can leap across empty space to catch one unawares. Many's the time those who watch begin to act in the same way. Then, they too must be purged—without mercy or hesitation.]

The fire's been lit. We see it, flicking multiple tongues into the night. Sparking and hissing. Spitting arcs of flame at the moon. It's imperative the village be kept bright, that all dark corners be banished. Both for us on these mountains and for the blacksmith's daughter. Invisible creatures with scarred red eyes creep along the edges of light, leaving the possibility of footprints. Searching for her. A howl. The blacksmith pauses for a moment on his stick's downward swing. Another. I shake my head beneath the torch. It's not my brother's howl. He can't erase completely the human element. My ears are tuned to his voice. When he could still talk, he kept mostly silent. Wandering about the village. Peering into windows. Smiling, head tilted. In the past few weeks, he has spoken to me often. But not tonight. Tonight, he's silent again. Or was I always interpreting senseless howls?

[The fiend takes whomever he wants whenever he wants. Except me. He can't take me. I've tried it. The tarantula, I mean. I've let it bite me repeatedly. Even in the most vulnerable spots, squirming with anticipated pain. But to no avail. In the end, it always crawls away in dejection, looking back balefully. Betrayed. Depleted. Nothing can deliver me to madness. To that state of simple bliss. When I do howl, it's not through some external force, some manic pressure. But only in response to my own will. I'll always be human. With no hope of joining my brother in a spontaneous duet.]

Blood red fingers of sun fade away across the gorse. Time to change direction. The young men perk up. Those from the other villages have come far enough. Their duty done, they head for the fire to await us. The rest of us turn one at a time. In this way surrounding the cave. Another formality. He won't run. The edges of my flesh tingle. I'm the lodestone, carrier of bad news and non-being. Fresh flowers were placed on my parents' grave this morning. In order to appease them. Forgive me, I whisper. Thick particles fly at me.

It's no use trying to lead the others astray. To some real wolf's den perhaps. Whose scarlet eyes would drive us into a frenzy. Would roll us down the mountain with the sticks becoming our worst enemies. No use. I'd always—at the last moment, at the last possible moment—point myself in the right direction.

[As a child, he ran through the streets in company with the stray dogs. Occasionally, I'd join in, but he knew I was there only to keep an eye on him.

The blacksmith's daughter had been promised him in marriage. They made a fine couple. So everyone said. Until he asked her to get down on all fours.]

Soon, soon. We'll catch sight of his cave. Small bones scattered across its entrance. Triangular piles no wolf could erect. But he hasn't killed these creatures whose bones he displays so gaudily. He only places them at the entrance to his cave in the belief it'll enhance his image before the other wolves. His tiny jaws aren't powerful enough to tear raw flesh. Except for nipples. We'll poke our smoking torches with caution into its mouth. Comfortable in the thought that fire decomposes the savage beast. Sends it exploding in all directions. We'll find him huddled in a corner of the cave. In the farthest, deepest corner amid stench and defecation. His body packed into the least volume possible. His hands over his head in an attitude of surrender. Urinating as well? We'll circle him. Tie him to a stick. Bind him like a wounded deer to the stick. He'll look up at me, eyes filled with pulsing veins, blood rushing to his head. I'll cry out not to hurt him as they wave the torches across his face and along the ridge of his spine. And then proceed to poke him myself.

[The worst. The most embarrassing. Was when he removed all his clothes. Dropped his pants at the least provocation. Then, he could always be found in the middle of a crowd. Doing tricks. Panting. Sniffing at their legs. I made efforts to cover him up but he always tore the clothing off as quickly as possible. In a blind rage as if he were being suffocated. I feared his being caught naked, appendages dangling. I feared his nakedness would lead to even more brutal behaviour on the part of his captors. On my part.]

We'll drop him roughly in the village square. An explosion of spittle and dust. And surround him as he's untied. Incantations circle in the air. They drop like bits of hot fat to scald flesh: "Demon, hie thee home!" "Get thee gone into the pit!" "Into the dark with thee and thy kind!" The blacksmith's wife will attack him with a bloodied axe. Only to be repelled by a hammer-blow from her husband. Our incantations—I'll scream the loudest, implore God the most—will be of no avail. Two of the braver men —from the next village—will tie his hands behind him. And pass the stick between his shoulder-blades. I'll be crying. I'll be sobbing. Memories of childhood will cascade from me and tumble into the fire. Will be charred by the flames. Will be spit out again in throbbing lumps of meat and gristle.

[The body of the blacksmith's daughter has been prepared. Those weeping against it no longer notice the powdered stain above her left breast. They're distracted by the fragrance of roses. The thick braids of garlic. The fact that soon she might be breathing again.]

The priest—the wizened priest—will emerge from his tiny chapel and bless the air. Someone is sneaking away to fornicate behind a hut. We'll turn our backs to the fire. Our shadows moving with the flames, playing crudely against the priest's vestments. For the first time, I'll feel a loathing, a disgust, for my brother. Here he is, being cleansed—"Leave the soul of this foul sinner, oh accursed demon. Make way for the bounty of the Lord." And he lies there. Motionless. Cowering. Not once howling. One howl. One howl and I'll fight the village for him. One howl and . . . nothing. Only a tinny yelping whenever the priest orders the demons to enter the boar tethered nearby to a grass rope. Thin and diseased. Squealing for mercy. No one but a blind fiend could be fooled into accepting such a poor substitute. Or no fiend. A god, perhaps, who takes the larded bones and leaves the meat.

I'll ask myself over and over why he isn't howling. What's wrong with him? The priest will drone on as we prod him. Push him. Close the circle. There's a demon here in the form of my brother. Animal grunts from behind a hut. I must push and prod him the hardest. His appearance is most deceiving. But he means nothing to me. Less than nothing. It's only a demon. Only a red-eyed, four-legged, forked-tailed . . . only a . . . With a moon-warping scream, the blacksmith will lift my brother into the air. High over his head. And hurl him into the fire. Something drops on the way. Falling from my brother's mouth. I crawl over to pick it up. Now the howls begin. The priest re-blesses the air. And turns away. The pig has been spared. Its owner can now offer it to God. The howls continue. They're not my brother's. He has no voice. The blacksmith's daughter will rise abruptly. Scream out last night's moon slicing the mountains and the stars crowning her head. There is a shout of joy. We've succeeded in cleansing her of the fiend's stain.

With the bloodless nipple in my mouth, knowing at last why my brother refused to howl, I'll scramble away. Falling over two spent bodies behind the hut. Rising again. Away from the fire. Whipping my fists into the air. Away from the fire that's searching for my eyes. Running. Scurrying down the snaky paths where a sharp stick waits. Impaled. Impaled by the giant who holds me wriggling in the air. I smile.

[But now, at this moment, at precisely this moment and at no other time, after slowly beating the bushes in search of his cave, I am standing over him, I am standing over my brother, I am standing frozen over my brother in the midst of a procession of torches, with both hands fastened to a stick lifted high, later to be used as a tomato stake, now at its peak, at its moment of descent, about to shard his skull, I am the giant reflected in his red eyes, at this moment, at exactly this moment, at no other.]

THE PHONE NUMBER

Geza Tatrallyay

The door to the container slid open and daylight crept in, assaulting Katya's still tired eyes. She raised her head as Eva stirred beside her on the bare mattress and she heard groans and sobs from the other girls who were waking to the sudden sunlight streaming in from outside. First one, then another male silhouette appeared as black shadows against the blinding brightness. As they moved inside, Katya immediately recognized Ivan the driver and then Rick, who seemed to be the contact man, in the entry.

"You there," Ivan shouted at someone over on the other side. "And you two." Now his gaze beckoned at Katya. "Come. We need to get you washed and dressed."

And when there was no response from the exhausted girls, Ivan made his way over to their mattress and grabbed Katya by the arm, pulled her up and shoved her toward the opening, before doing the same to Eva.

"Yes, my dear, you have some work to do again this afternoon," Katya heard the rasping voice of the one called Rick, still over by the entrance. "Get your ass over here, babe. You gotta earn your keep."

It had been Rick who had recruited her into this terrible mess, masquerading as an agent from the University of Florida offering very selective scholarships. It had all sounded so, so tempting, and stupidly, she had fallen for it.

Katya moved hesitantly toward Rick, who grabbed her as soon as she was within reach and, twisting her arm, tugged her down the ramp toward the little building beside which the container had been placed.

"Okay, you stupid bitch, get inside and wash up and put some clean clothes on. You'll find everything you need in there."

Katya knew she had no choice. If she resisted, she knew that the punishment would be hell. Could be serial rape by all four of the minders, or hanging naked from a hook in the ceiling of the container all night, on tiptoes, being abused mentally and physically, or both. But no marks, at least there was that. They wanted to keep the girls intact for the customers.

Or like Anna, who disappeared after God only knows what they did to her. No, she had to stop thinking about it. She had to go along with what they said for now, but she needed to find a way to escape.

And there was a ray of hope, as of last evening. The phone number. 1-888-373-7888.

Katya had finally fallen asleep the night before as she was going over the phone number that she had seared in her memory earlier that day when she had been delivered in a van to a hotel to be with another customer. Right after the creep had maneuvered her into the bedroom, she had gone to the bathroom on the pretext of needing to empty herself, but really to gain time to think and prepare herself mentally for what would inevitably come next. There, beside the granite sink, she had been surprised to see the piece of soap with the number "1-888-373-7888" and the words

"National Human Trafficking Hotline" under it, marked on the wrapper. She had quickly committed the number to memory and flushed the wrapper down the toilet—certainly, she didn't want the beast out there, or, worse still, any of her minders to see it. She delayed for as long as she could in the bathroom to go over the telephone number, but when the man started to shake the door, she knew she no longer had any choice.

As she stripped and reluctantly satisfied the pervert, Katya hoped that once done, she would have a chance to use the phone by the bedside, or if not, then steal the man's mobile, but there had been no opportunity. Her handlers came promptly and they and the man gave her no privacy. They shoved her around and slapped her on the rear before the gangsters whisked her back to the container where the trafficked girls were kept for the duration of the Super Bowl. That night, though, she whispered the number to Eva, the only girl she trusted now that Anna was gone. Perhaps they would find a way to make a call to the hotline.

Yes, that number would be her salvation. She would get to a phone somehow. Maybe today. The sooner the better.

Showered, dressed and made-up, Katya and Eva and a third girl they barely knew—Trish, an American teenager, she thought—were shoved by Ivan and Rick into the back of a white van with no windows. Ivan drove for about half an hour, Katya guessed, before they pulled off the road and then, after a few turns, brought the van to a halt.

"God, I hope this will not be as terrible as the last time," Trish whined, barely able to hold the tears back. Outside, they heard Rick greet some men, and after some jovial exchanges they couldn't make out, the van door opened.

"Come on girls, time to perform," Rick said. "The customers are waiting."

The girls slowly clambered out of the back of the van and into the sunlight. Five men were standing there, all with hungry, leering expressions.

"Wow!" Katya heard the smallest pervert utter. "They sure are beauts, just like you said."

"Have fun you guys," Rick yelled, as he got back in the passenger seat of the van. We'll be back to pick them up in six hours."

A big hulk with his shirt open revealing a hairy chest and a large gut moved toward Katya, grabbed her by the arm and said, "This one is mine. At least I get first dibs."

"No fair, Jeb, we said we would toss a coin."

"Fuck that, Lenny, you should be glad I let you come along. The other two are not bad either. And we'll trade later, don't worry. You'll get your turn if you can still get it up."

The man called Jeb twisted Katya's arm behind her and tugged the frightened girl through the large living room of the luxurious villa and into a huge bedroom with a king-size bed, whipping her around to face him as he started pawing her. Katya tried to wriggle away, but he grabbed at her, tearing her blouse and ripping her miniskirt off her. He whirled her around and shoved her down on the bed.

To put off the agony, as the brute started to undress, Katya turned around and pleaded, "I need to go to the bathroom. Please. Before . . ."

Jeb looked at her with disgust and then said, "Okay, you stupid bitch. But take your bra off first and make it fast."

Katya quickly got up, did as she was told and, covering her breasts as best she could, made her way to the bathroom. Jeb yelled after her, "Don't lock the fucking door, you cunt."

Shaking, she nevertheless pulled the door shut and went to sit down on the toilet, burying her face in her hands. The terrible thought entered her mind that after Jeb, there were still several other men out in the living room no doubt waiting to get at her. There were more of the horny revellers than the three girls provided by the gang—five or six of them she thought. Trish and Eva had been coerced into entertaining the others with an erotic dance à deux while the hairy bully, this Jeb who had claimed first dibs, would have his way with her.

She thought of the soap and the number and that gave her strength. Finishing, she gingerly opened the door and the hairy beast, gut hanging over his filthy boxers, immediately grabbed her, twisted her around and reached down inside her panties, ripping them off with brute force. He whipped her back around and tried to plant his alcohol-reeking mouth on hers. She tried to resist but knew full well that there was no way she could avoid what came next. As she struggled, Katya glanced around to see if there was a phone anywhere. But Jeb quickly dragged her over to the bed and pushed her face down into the pillows, yelling, "What the fuck were you doing in there for so long, you stupid Russian cunt? Playing with your clit? I'll teach you . . ."

Katya kept reciting 3737 to herself, sure she would remember the 888s on either side, as Jeb forced himself into her from behind and stifled her scream with a sweaty hand clamped over her mouth. She knew she had to endure this horror, live through it as best she could. She tried to think ahead to the aftermath when she would have to find the strength to rummage through the lowlife's clothes for his cellphone—since there didn't seem to be a fixed line in this posh villa, certainly not in this bedroom—just as soon as he released her and hopefully disappeared into the bathroom to wash himself. And it would all have to be done very quickly.

Katya was in tears from the pain and humiliation as the fat slob finally finished doing his thing and slowly got off her, slapping her hard on the buttocks.

"Well done, babe," Jeb said, with a little laugh. "You sure are a great fuck. Even though you are one stupid Russian cunt." He slid off the bed, looked down at his condom-covered member, picked up his boxers and made his way to the bathroom as he chuckled,

"Yuck! I guess I'd better wash myself off."

As soon as the monster closed the bathroom door—in spite of the pain she felt down below—Katya got up and started to go through the clothes that were thrown in a pile on a chair. Sure enough, she found a cell phone in the pants' pocket and hoped that it was not locked. But just as she was about to check, someone knocked on the bedroom door and yelled, "Hey Jeb, you jerk-off! What the fuck is taking you so long? Give us other guys a turn." And then, after a pause, "or maybe two of us should do it at the same time, eh? Double tag her. How about it?"

And as Jeb flushed the toilet, Katya jumped back on the bed, shoved the mobile under the mattress and tried to assume the same position she had been in before, all the time continuing to sob, but managing to pull the duvet over her aching body. As she did so, she noticed the blood down the back of her thighs and on the sheets. Sure enough, Jeb lumbered over to the bedroom door and as he unlocked it, Katya hoped that he would not notice that his clothes had been gone through and that his phone was gone. If he did, that would be the end of her.

"Well, well, so you horny guys want to have a turn with this cunt, do you? Do come in, do come in ..."

"Jeb, fuck it. You can't just monopolize the best babe in town, you dickhead. You can bet your fat ass we want a turn."

"Yeah, this one is a hottie all right," Jeb remarked as he pulled the duvet off Katya, exposing her to the view of the others.

The guy at the door yelled back into the living room, "Hey, who wants to do a duo with the hot blonde chick Jeb just made?"

Someone shouted back, "With you, Bob, you shithead? Not on your life . . ." as another partyer appeared. "Jesus, Jeb, why the fuck don't you get her to wash herself? She's got your scum and sweat all over her bod—and is that blood down there? What the fuck did you do to her, you asshole? I ain't goin' near the bitch until she washes."

"Did you hear what my friend said—what the fuck's your name—Katya? Get up and go wash yourself. And don't close the door, because we all want to watch."

Katya just lay there not moving, thinking this time disobedience may be her best strategy. Besides, she was glad to be immobile—that way the pain was more or less tolerable.

"Shit, Jeb," the guy called Bob came closer, "did you fucking kill the twat?" He grabbed her wrist, and after a moment said, "Well, at least she has a pulse. Maybe we just need to let her rest a mo. Let's go and play with the other two babes meanwhile."

The three slobs left the room, but they left the door open a crack. Katya did not move as she listened to the sounds from the other room, glad to be left alone.

"Come on, baby," she heard from afar one of the men say a moment later, "it's time for blow jobs all around! Both of you, come on, show us what you can do with your fucking lips and tongues."

"Yeah, great stuff!" Katya heard Bob say. "Get your ass over here, Eva, and get on it."

She tried to close her ears to this disgusting banter and sounds, and concentrate on her next move. She figured she would have maybe fifteen minutes—maybe one or two more—if all the men were going to join in whatever was going on next door.

Katya started to feel around for the phone hidden under the mattress and as soon as her right hand locked on it, she maneuvered her body out of the bed as gently and as quietly as possible. She moved quickly to the bathroom, holding the cell between her breasts and away from the door to the living room. Katya closed the bathroom door quietly, locking it so the brutes would have to break it down to get to her. She sat on the toilet, opened the phone and was devastated when she saw that it needed a pin number or a thumbprint. The realization that she would not be able to call the National Trafficking Hotline brought her to tears. But then . . . at the bottom of the screen she noticed the word "Emergency." With her shaking finger, she pressed that corner and put the phone to her ear, hoping that this would work.

Indeed, she was relieved when a reassuring female voice came on the line with an urgent "911, what's your emergency?"

And then, when Katya did not say anything, the woman continued, "Please, can you tell me what is wrong . . . Where are you?"

"I am somewhere . . . big house . . . in bathroom. We are being trafficked . . . horribly abused. Two other girls. We were brought here to have . . . sex with awful men."

"What is your name?"

"Katya . . . Gusov."

"Who else is in the house, Katya?"

"Eva Baransky. And . . . Trish . . . I don't know name. Six men . . . terrible men. We brought here by gang . . . they brought us from Florida . . . in truck. They rent us for sex to these men. These . . . perverts . . . do horrible things. Please . . ."

"Katya, is there anything else you can tell us to help us find the house?"

"It is, I think, rented. Some villa . . . pretty . . . how do you say it . . . posh. Other times we kept in container by gang. Maybe . . . twenty-five minutes or half an hour from here. They bring us here in van. These men already at villa. Oh, please help us!"

"Katya, I know this is dangerous for you, but you need to keep talking to me for just a little longer. We are locating where you are and every second helps. Now, do you know any names?"

"Just Jeb, I think," Katya said between sobs. "And there is Bob and I don't know . . ."

There was a scream that penetrated through the two doors. Katya wondered what those animals were doing to Eva and Trish.

"Please, please, hurry! I am so afraid . . . I must put cellphone back in man's pockets now . . . I took it from pants he left on chair."

"Katya, you mention the gang . . . did the men who brought you here . . . did they have an accent?" the 911 woman asked.

"Yes, some did. Russian. They spoke to me in Russian. Some others American . . ."

"Okay, Katya, you've done great . . . we have a pinpoint. We're on our way. Hold out just a little longer, dear."

Katya was shaking as she turned the mobile off. She grabbed a tissue to wipe the tears from her eyes, quickly washed herself and unlatched the door, quietly opening it. She listened a moment to the sounds emanating from the living room—moaning and groaning, grunting and panting, an occasional slap followed by a wince or a scream. She rapidly made her way over to the chair where Jeb's clothes were in a messy pile, and with hands shaking, put the phone back in the pocket she had found it.

As Katya was collecting what was left of her torn clothes, she heard a voice—was it Bob—say, "Hey, it seems your cunt, Jeb, is finally back in the world of the living. I just heard some noises from next door."

"Well, let's get her in here to join in the fun. We haven't seen what the bitch can do with those beautiful lips of hers, have we, guys? Her ass certainly was quite something."

Katya recoiled as she heard a high-pitched squeak say, "I'll go get her," and quickly ran back toward the bathroom.

"Okay, Lenny. It's probably your turn anyway."

The little man called Lenny appeared in the bedroom just as Katya slammed the bathroom door shut and locked it. She leaned against it, slumped to the floor and assumed a fetal position, saying, "No, no. No, please no."

From the other side, she heard Lenny yell, "Hey, the bitch just locked herself in the fucking bathroom."

"Well, break the door down, you idiot."

"Yeah, we can't let her get away with it. The stupid cunt has only put out for Jeb. We got to get our fucking money's worth."

"Okay. Okay. I'll see what I can do." With this, Lenny slammed his shoulder into the door and Katya could feel it rattle and shake. But it held. She needed it to hold until the police came.

"Shit! The fucking thing is solid."

"Okay, okay. You pussy. I'll come in a second. You're useless anyway, you little cunt," Jeb grumbled.

Katya heard someone fall, then crying and surmised it was Trish, by far the youngest of the girls. "You have no tits and no butt. And you just can't move your fucking lips fast enough. We're gonna get our money back for sure."

"Come on, Jeb."

"Okay, Lenny let's both put our shoulders to this fucking door. One, two, three . . . ho."

The door gave just a little. But it held.

"Again!" It still held.

"Fuck!" Jeb said, pissed off. "Come on, Lenny, let's really do it."

And this time the doorjamb broke. The two slobs came crashing through the opening, Lenny falling on top of Katya where she was against the far wall, trembling. As Jeb recovered and pulled her out from under his buddy, he said, "Come on, babe, it's time for you to service little Lenny here. And my other friends next door."

Back in the bedroom, the weasel called Lenny pulled his member out and started working it as Jeb forced Katya to her knees in front of him, tearing her already torn T-shirt off again.

At that very moment, there was a big crash, as one of the picture windows in the living room was smashed to smithereens and a posse of cops broke through in full battle gear with automatics pointed at the men in the midst of their lewd activities. Two of the policemen appeared at the bedroom door as Jeb released Katya, who flopped to the floor.

"Okay, don't anybody move! Let the girl go."

Lenny, with his boxers down at his ankles, said, "Oh, no!" while Jeb just said, "Shit!" as they both raised their hands. Katya gingerly stood up and, covering her breasts with her arms, moved toward the police, casting an eye back toward her tormentors.

"Thank you. Thank you," were the only words she could utter to the police as she was overwhelmed by her tears—of pain, of suffering, of humiliation but mostly of relief.

"You're safe now, honey," Katya heard a woman say from the door to the living room. "Come, sit here beside your friend." Still trembling, Katya went over to the couch and hugged a weeping, bruised and naked Eva. The female agent found a blanket somewhere and handed it to the girls to cover up. Still unable to shed her fear, Katya watched as Jeb and Lenny and the other perverts were led away handcuffed to the police cars outside. Slowly though, she felt the warmth of hope envelope her—hope that indeed her ordeal as a trafficked woman was over.

Many young women worldwide are trafficked for sex by ruthless gangs. Major sports events that attract male fans, such as the Super Bowl, World Cup, the Olympics and top golf and tennis competitions, are prime venues for these traffickers to carry out their sordid business. To fight human trafficking, some public and civic groups have mounted a widespread effort focusing especially on such events to promulgate a National Human Trafficking Hotline 1-888-373-7888 created and operated in the US by Polaris, a non-profit, non-governmental entity. These efforts have included the placement of bars of soap and makeup wipes with the number on the wrapper in hotel bathrooms as well as the distribution and placement of card and posters in hotel lobbies. They have had good success, resulting in just short of 54,000 calls in 2016. A similar hotline is now being implemented in Canada by the Canadian Centre to End Human Trafficking, and this will came into operation in the spring of 2019. In addition, most cellphones now have a feature so that emergency calls can be placed free of charge from anywhere without the need to unlock the phone.

This short story is a humble effort to help publicize the hotline and to illustrate graphically the life-saving benefits that these measures are having.

ON FIRE BRIDGE

Ursula Pflug

I'M SURE NOW THAT you started the fires, that your desire called them into being.

I see you in our kitchen, your orange-stockinged legs up on the table, smoking cigarettes, pleased as punch. It's dawn and we haven't slept.

"We are like gods," you say, "playing marbles in space." I like you saying it. I like your arrogance. I like how you always push me to stay up late, when, if it was up to me, I'd have been in bed hours ago. But you need those sunrises, need what they give you.

We walked together so very far, little friend, much farther than I ever could've gone without you. I was so happy! We dreamed together, prying open all the doors in space, doors that were never supposed to be opened, at least not by us. The revolutions that occurred in far corners of the galaxy because of our pliers!

Revolutions that were never supposed to occur, at least not for that reason. In the very centre of things we found a gaping hole and fell into it. Time yawned. In its breath, we were taken apart and reassembled, exquisitely, in a different way.

IN MY MEMORY, I COME with you till halfway across the bridge. It is so cold on your damn bridge, a shivering place, and underneath us the waters rage, a stormy winter current so strong I'm afraid it will carry me away, even when I'm just looking at it. I never thought for a moment you were planning a much longer journey, a journey you would never return from. I come up behind you, always the dawdler, going only because you have gone, although sometimes you fool me, allowing me to believe it is I who leads.

On the bridge I stay back a few feet, watching, a little terrified, how you sit on the edge, your legs dangling, staring into the whirlpools. I like it, but it's very strong, enough of God's raw breath to last me a whole month. But you, you always want to stay. You call me a wimp. All the same, you want me with you. When we do leave, you explain, it's because of me because you don't want to stay alone. I sigh. We go home together, home to breakfast specials and laundry and floors that always get dirty again. I am content just to be with you, but for you, there is never enough; you are so hungry, always wanting to go back. Over morning coffees we argue, and the outcome is always the same. You will go alone, you say, if I don't come.

Until I met you I thought I was the brave one, the adventurer, and sometimes you even let me believe it, for a little while, so long as it meant I'd come a little further, stay a little longer. Until of course the time came I didn't go. And now I retrace our worn steps, calling, hoping to find you.

THE SURFACE OF THE WATER rippling. Scudding smoke, embers. The fire is close by tonight. The rain turns cold, turns white.

Pebbly stone rough under my hands. The bridge's railing. One hand, the right one, curled around a cigarette. Cigarettes change taste when it turns cold, when the snow comes. The new sharp smell reminds me of you. I smoke. The tips of my fingers go numb and tingly with clues. You are nearby.

And now this writing has led me to you, to a voice that seems to be yours, to a place like the places you loved, the bridges. "Isn't it good here?" you say in my mind. "Isn't it good?"

And I say, "God, how I've missed you, how I've missed this strange feeling, as though my cells were electrified, as though I'd been drinking for a week, as though I hadn't slept in years. Oh God, oh God," I say.

You chide me, saying, "If only you'd come too, that last time like you promised, everything would have been different."

Perhaps I did promise.

If only I'd had the courage to leap into the fire, then I would find you still alive, unsinged. I go in my mind, now, just for a moment, to be with you. You are always inside the fire now, dancing. It's as if I can see you through the flames, as though you come out and join me to say, "Hey, no burn marks."

We talk. I care about burned bridges, about writing, but you never have. "It doesn't matter," you say, "death doesn't matter, appearances are a lie. They saw insanity, those others, but that was only the outer shell. I am where I have always been, dancing inside the fire." Ah, that strange feeling of being with you.

It's always night and sleeting on your bridge.

You turn to go. You smile, will I cross with you tonight? But I don't, not even this time, this second chance. If I did, they'd burn the bridge, and besides, I have to be somewhere in the morning, to write you into life. I stroke your leather jacket good-bye, with a tenderness born of fear, as though even in this dream our lives are so dangerous we might really never see one another again. As perhaps they are.

My footsteps ring on the empty bridge, but you call me back one more time.

"Kim?"

And I say, "Yes?" and you hand me a film can, full of wooden matches.

"You might need them later," you say when I ask.

IN THE MORNING, THE CITY is grey and full of rain. I walk through it bleakly, missing you. The newspaper is full of stories of fires, and I am jealous, knowing you caused them. I go to the bridge, but in the morning it is just a bridge, snow swirling into the river. There is the smell of smoke, of fire, but I know that even if I crossed here, I'd never be able to find you; the snow has obscured your footsteps. Still, I hear you laughing at me, faint as a train whistle, very far away. Later on, I sit in cafés and look out at the snow. I drink coffee and smoke endlessly, writing in notebooks, feeling I have failed.

THE FORGETTING BEGINS, THE LOSS of memory. For days that feel like centuries, I sit in my diner by the river, reading my newspapers, watching the snow swirl. I forget what you look like; everyone becomes you. They build a highway, a busy one, between the diner and the river; all summer the bulldozers are hungry, tearing the earth. When winter comes again I have finished the front section, moved on to arts and entertainment. When the snow returns I am sure you will come back, will bloom again like a winter flower. I bring a boom box to the diner, and I listen to talk shows and to my favourite tapes while I wait for my pancakes. When they close up for the night they leave one light on for me and let me help myself to coffee. I become a legend, a tourist attraction; bohemians and artsy types come and sit down beside me, hoping to catch some of my fire, hoping they, too, will become so free they will be allowed to stay in diners all night long, watching the fish swim around the room at purple morning, let out from their aquarium for an hour at dawn before the place opens for the nine-to-fivers to get there before work coffees.

PURPLE CHRYSANTHEMUMS APPEAR IN MY water glass, books on my table, television sets. Soon they move out the next table to replace it with a washer and dryer; after the showers are installed I never have to leave. Still, I forget you. Still, I see others. A man with long yellow hair tied back with a string shares my table for weeks; he shares my ability to go without sleep, or else he's the only one I know who can drink as much coffee as I. He makes tiny objects so small one needs a microscope to see them, but his hands are like laser beams and he can work without one, so one learns his trick and one's own eyes become microscopes too. Tiny sections of the table become very large, magnified a thousand times, until one can see them, the things he makes: intricate boxes full of electronic parts and food for the soul. They are beautiful, they are art.

Then, slowly, I begin to remember. I don't remember what it is I have forgotten, just a nagging sensation in the thighs. I stare at a man in the phone booth, his hand cupped around the receiver. Is it you? But the question is meaningless because I have forgotten who you are supposed to be, what it is you do, only (and until recently I didn't know even this) that once you existed; now you do not. The blonde man has moved on, but yet another stranger, this time with short dark hair, comes in and piles his knapsack on the floor under my table. He goes to the bathroom, and I get up to do his laundry; in the pockets of his jeans, I find maps, maps and names.

For the first time in three years, I leave the diner. I call a number I found in the stranger's pocket, on the same page as a map of a bridge. A woman answers, her voice breezy and sincere. Suddenly I know where she lives. It is a house I once stayed in with you. She didn't live there then; there were others; we didn't know them well. We'd sit around the kitchen table reading science fiction books (everyone in that house read science fiction), comparing plots and styles of writing, bitching about the price of cigarettes, the price of time. Whenever I was with you, it was always someone else's kitchen. In this memory which is not a real one but one invented by the telephone wires, one which cannot exist independently of them, you are going away somewhere, and I am sad. Through the smoke of the cooking, the cigarettes, the people, you smile the smile of a brother and I am comforted.

"I'll be back," you say.

But you weren't. In that life, you never came back. Or I waited for you in the wrong place, on the wrong bridge. When I hang up the phone I am released from the invented life, the life that never happened except in the electronic part of memory that exists because of telephones and computers, but I am still left with the nagging suspicion that you are real, that somewhere I will find a real memory of you. So I go to the bridge; it snows; I wait for you. I do not know if this is the right bridge, but it is the only bridge I know.

YOU DIED IN THE FIRE. But that was in another city, and you and I both had different names then. Maybe in this city I have moved to, this emerald green city below the border, you will have a new name, one that doesn't burn so easily. Maybe in this city, we will meet on the bridge. They do not know, those artists, that this freedom I have is not mine. They do not know I have it only because of you.

I remember how I used to visit you and you would tell me you wished for drugs and shock treatments, how it would make you happy, because then you could no longer think and see and feel, and that would be better. "But that would mean being stupid," I said, and you said it would be better. "But that would mean happiness was only possible if you were stupid," and again you said it would be better.

Sometimes it is as though all of love died with you in that fire. I couldn't bear it, so I tried to escape, hoping even the memory of you could disappear in this fog. And now it begins to be not you I mourn, but someone else whose name I can never place, someone whose loss I mourn more than all the others, someone whom my human lovers can only approximate, be representations of.

PATSY CLINE SINGS SONGS OF LOVE

Sang Kim

You'd think they'd recognize my voice by now. The operator on the other end instructs me to stand closer to the intercom, say my name again in both English and Korean. When the tinted glass door slides open, a young nurse in green scrubs is already waiting for me on the other side, looking annoyed.

—*Sorry. The traffic.*

He turns and walks ahead, motioning his hand in the air like he is wiping chalk off a board—I've prolonged his shift. I follow him upstairs into her room where a vaguely Victorian wrought-iron grill's been installed outside her window.

—*Thank you.*

He nods again without looking at me and closes the door behind him.

She's two floors down, in the garden, slumped in a wheelchair, her face wrapped in gauze. She leans forward when something catches her eyes on the other side of the brook. A dogwood shrub that may or may not be the face of Satan or God, or a burning bush. She opens and closes her mouth and slumps back into her chair again. I walk away from the window when she tilts her head toward the building.

ON HER NIGHTSTAND ARE MASON jars of specimens suspended in formaldehyde—amniotic in colour, as if drawn from some primordial swamp. The bloated white belly of a splayed bullfrog; two small koi—one orange one black, a yin and yang. A vampire bat stares out through filmy eyes at the newspaper clipping tacked on the opposite wall. The one of her. *Woman Caught Running Wild Through High Park*. She's about fifteen feet ahead of the photographer, head cocked to the side like a distressed hen. Buck-naked except for the blackened sole of her right sock. The bones in her back and the bottom of her rib cage stick out through slick near-translucent skin. Her soaked hair, unkempt from six days in that church basement, sprang from her head like Medusa's snakes.

Casting out the devil is God's law, not Man's.

Pastor Kwak was impenitent to the end.

She rested a hand on the Bible the whole time, never once responded to the prosecutor's promptings. The judge instructed her to tell the court.

—Tell the court about what happened, the translator told my mother.

So she told the translator what happened to Patsy Cline.

같은 날, 6월 14일, 그녀는 정면 충돌에 관여했습니다. 테네시 내쉬빌에있는 Old Hickory Boulevard 에서 일어난 일입니다. 그녀는 머리를 앞 유리에 박살 내고 거의 죽었다. 한 달 후, 그녀가 병원을 떠날 때, 그녀는 그녀의 이마와 예수님의 가슴에 상처를 가지고있었습니다... 이 비행기는 Piper PA-24 Comanche (등록 번호 N-7000P) 입니다. 그것은 오후 6시 7 분에 테네시 주 디어스 버그에서 출발하여 내쉬빌에서 140 킬로미터 떨어진 곳에서 발견되었습니다. Patsy 의 손목 시계를 발견했을 때 오후 6시 20

분에 멈췄습니다.

That same day, June fourteenth, she was involved in a head-on car crash. It happened on Old Hickory Boulevard in Nashville, Tennessee. She smashed her head into the windshield and almost died. One month later, when she left the hospital, she had a scar on her forehead and Jesus in her heart. The plane was a Piper PA-24 Comanche, registration number N-7000P. It took off from Dyersburg, Tennessee at 6:07 p.m. and was found 140 kilometers from Nashville, nose down. When they found Patsy's wristwatch, it had stopped at 6:20 pm.

Pastor Kwak was granted conditional discharge, released the same day.

That night, we took her to her favourite Japanese restaurant on Bloor, sushi served on a rotating conveyor belt around the perimeter of the bar. She passed on the prized tuna sashimi and sea bream *nigiri*, watched a young couple at the end of the bar pick them up with glee.

The tongue serves five functions: mastication, deglutition or swallowing, oral cleansing, and assisting in the identification of taste. Apart from those biological functions, it plays a critical role in the articulation of sound. A partially-damaged tongue distorts patterns of speech. But when most of the tongue is removed, speech becomes near impossible.

Doctor Noh's hands are tucked in the pockets of her wool blazer. She is all business. It's only when she passes me my mother's request, scrawled in red crayon on a scrap of paper, that I hear a meager inflection of sympathy in her voice. Now, looking down at the garden, even she knows we have been plunged into uncharted waters. She turns to tell me the speech pathologist is waiting for us in her office.

THE FIRST TIME SHE WAS admitted here, I filled out her medical history questionnaire. One answer required an "Explain Further" box, just big enough for a thumbprint.

Symptoms only appeared after seven years in the country. No indication of trauma at the refugee camp. I was too young to remember anything from the war.

In the Rec Room, through the wire glass window, a man's standing on a makeshift platform, holding a microphone too close to his mouth, making throaty sounds. Behind him, white Korean script appears and fades away on a rose-coloured screen.

나는 너를 정말로 사랑해
너는 나를 떠난 후 내가 얼마나
많이 울었는지 모르겠다

He's being watched by an elderly woman in a Hello Kitty nightgown, arms wrapped around her knees, rocking. He might be deaf.

The night before it happened, she recorded the song on *Side A* of the cassette in this very room, speaking over the opening lines:

—*Are you ready? I'm ready.*

The audience applauds. There's whistling, the occasional hoot. She slips into the second line without missing a beat. By the third, her voice has merged with Patsy's. Each word off her tongue a gentle cascade that finishes with a purr. The audience knows the song well, joins in on the chorus. But the final two lines are all hers—*a cappella,* no accompaniment, in a lower register. It comes at you unexpectedly, like two puncture wounds, raw, almost painful. When it's over, in the crowded hush, she speaks softly into the microphone.

—*Don't forget. Patsy Cline sings songs of love.*

And that's it. End of the recording.

It wasn't a tongue specialist who performed the surgery. There were none in the Orangeville area at the time. Doctor Noh taps lightly on her own office door before turning the knob.

What is unclear at this time is the pharmacodynamic interaction between the post-operative medication and the drugs used to treat her other disorders. What remained of the tongue was infected by contaminants in the glass.

Aileen, the speech pathologist, is standing when we enter, focused on a moving spot on the floor. Her hand's clammy and when she sits back down, I resist looking at the mason jar on the desk behind her. She doesn't want to be here or pities me, I can't tell which. When she is asked to speak by Doctor Noh, she fidgets with her flip chart.

Given the state of what remains of her tongue and her mental condition, speech therapy is not recommended at this time.

On *Side B*, she tells the story of Patsy's near-death experience after a bout with rheumatic fever. One night after a seemingly harmless throat infection, her heart stopped beating. Her parents rushed her to the hospital where doctors resuscitated her and kept her alive in an oxygen tent. When she returned to the living several days later, she launched her singing career.

—Can you believe that? An oxygen tent! Millions of molecules bouncing off each other.

Someone enters the room. It is Nuri, her floormate, the one who's jumped out of her own window twice. She is anxious.

—*Unni.*

—*Can't you see I'm talking to my son?*

My mother is fiddling with something. It sounds like the metal lid of a mason jar.

—*It's back. In my bathroom.*

—*Tell the nurses. I'm busy right now.*

—*They won't listen to me.*

—*If you don't think about it, it can't hurt you. Okay? All. In. Your. Head.*

I imagine her jabbing her index finger on the lid.

—*I swear, it's not in my head. I saw it.*
—*Get out of my room! Get out!*

She grunts. Something is hurled against a wall. Glass shatters. Nuri screams. The door slams. Moments later, she is speaking again into the recorder, sentences so quick they're run-on gibberish, followed by stammering with hard nasal consonants stabbing the air.

Suddenly it's quiet. Slippers along the floor. Shifting glass. There's a pause followed by gagging, then gargling. More feet. Gasps. A shrill shout for a first aid kit. Someone on the phone demanding an ambulance. Glass cracking under shoes.

—*My god, my god . . .*

The recording ends there.

SHE IS WHEELED IN BY the same male nurse. I try to feel for him, try to imagine somebody who loves him waiting at home, a napkin laid over his dinner to keep it warm. He leaves without acknowledging Doctor Noh's thank you. Maybe he's like the singer in the Rec Room. Maybe he's deaf.

The bruises around her mouth and nose are primary—blue and yellow and red. I am reminded of that time, when my father was still alive, the three of us lying on crunchy snow and watching the Northern Lights. One week ago she still looked like the mother who squeezed my hand when the lights flickered against that cold glassy sky. But now, her eyes glazed over from the narcotics, it's only when she sees the mason jar on the desk that her eyes dilate. She grips the wheels of her chair, maneuvers awkwardly towards it. She can't quite reach so she turns toward me with moist, almost lucid eyes. Her arm raised, index finger extended toward the jar. When she tries to talk, the soiled gauze around her chin stretches, and I think of a duck's webbed feet. I crumple the scrap of paper Doctor Noh gave me in my hand and wish she would stop. I want to give her what she wants, but not that. I can't move. And I can't turn away. Some urge keeps me staring at her mouth, that gaping black hole, the primary-coloured bruises around it, the spit mixed with blood between her lips. I know I need her to utter something, anything, to salvage some shred of hope still flapping inside me. I close my eyes for a flicker, bite down hard on my tongue, and for a moment I'm disgusted with myself and I don't know why.

There against the clamped red screens of my eyelids white Korean characters fade in and out. And then I hear it, that voice with the warm hand on that cold brittle night, beckoning, calling out breathlessly: *Oh, look. Over there, look at those colours.*

It sounds like Patsy Cline. It feels like love.

THE WEDDING

Timothy Niedermann

As HE WALKED TOWARD the home of Abu Nasir, Hanif thought of a conversation he had had with Rashid a couple of years earlier. Hanif's son was wondering why he had returned to their village from his time abroad, why he had never chosen to live in a city like perhaps Ramallah or even leave Palestine altogether for a new life, a new adventure somewhere else.

"Why do you stay? This is such a small place. I look around, and I don't see many opportunities for young people like me. And everybody knows each other's business. It's so confining! We have relatives in Europe and North America. You could have found a job somewhere else easily. So why? Why did you come back?"

Hanif had shaken his head. The ferocity of the teenage mind! He remembered feeling the same way once, though. Indeed, he had lived in Europe for part of his schooling. But yes, he had returned. He had tried to explain why to Rashid.

"When I was abroad, I enjoyed myself. I certainly learned a lot. But after the first few months I felt something was missing. Lots of things, really. The familiar things. I would go on walks and want to be walking on my own land, my people's land. The rhythms of life are different everywhere, and I found I prefer the rhythms here, I guess. Perhaps it's as simple as that."

But of course it wasn't. The choice had been difficult. In the end, his decision to come back to Palestine was emotional rather than rational, a product of visceral need, not impartial calculation. What was it that made him return—to reject the experiment of living in a new place, experiencing new cultures, new people, new everything? Perhaps it was because the village was not just home but his family, containing all those things that nourish and give solace. Can foreign lands supply that? He thought not.

There were other conversations, of course. Arguments. That's what teenagers do. Hanif not only accepted that, he prized it. His son was demanding. Rashid wanted to know truth. He didn't accept what many said as rote, as dictated. Hanif was proud, so proud of Rashid for that.

The struggle over traditions had continued. Traditions can evolve. Hanif knew this. They sustain a person, a people. They give a base, a feeling of solidity. Anyone's life needs that. But here, it was truly difficult. The Occupation was an assault on everything they had, everything they valued. How do you keep your traditions in such a situation? Some tried resistance, others tried to find ways to dig deeper roots to hold firm. But for others, it meant that their attachment to the land was weakened and starved. Hanif could see it erode and desiccate his people. Everyone was affected, especially the young. For Rashid and young people like him, the world outside beckoned stronger, each passing year.

"I'll create new traditions. I'll build on the old, on the past, and create something new in a new country. Something for the twenty-first century. Something for me and my children to pass on. I promise." Rashid was adamant and sincere.

On one level, Hanif had to agree. Traditions had to change, had to adapt to the times. Was he, Hanif, being too rigid, too backward looking? Was he looking backward to a halcyon, maybe mythical past, or was he just stubborn, too set in his ways? He wasn't sure.

But now Rashid was to have a traditional Palestinian wedding. The date had been set, and so, in the time-honoured way, Hanif, as the father of the groom, had gone from door to door in the village to invite every household to take part. This naturally took several days. He was often invited in, given coffee, and made to share pleasantries with whoever was home. And where he found nobody in, he had to return. No one was to be left out. No one. So it took time.

The visits were often long, and often more than not a bit repetitive. But that's the way villages can be, lives overlap in so many ways. Yet always there was something special, a unique anecdote about Dalia or Rashid that only that person had experienced. A warm connection with the two.

The couple, of course, was well known to all. Since they were little children they had attracted the attention, and judgements, of the village.

"How old were they then? When they first met. He couldn't have been more than sixteen. Maybe only fifteen. She was a few months younger. Probably you didn't know, but they walked home together after school. Sometimes they held hands. So adorable."

The things neighbours know and parents don't, at least not immediately.

Of course childhood romances seldom last, so at the time neither he nor Marwa, his wife, had thought much of it. But they trusted their son's sense of propriety. More importantly, so did Dalia's parents it seemed. And village life is not like the city. Nothing is really anonymous or private. People are always watching you, not maliciously, but because they know you, they feel you are a part of them, a member of a family, however extended. And like everyone else in the village, Hanif knew that there had been secret meetings in one olive grove or another, and unsupervised parties at friend's houses when the parents were away. All normal. He remembered his own youth with a smile.

Trust, though, is a wonderful thing when confirmed, and it was such a compliment to have his best hopes in his son justified.

Dalia, too, was trustworthy. She was what people used to call a "sensible" girl, meaning at once both polite and not emotional. Careful. Not naïve the way some girls can be when they discover boys. So the two families had become friends as well. Perhaps that had helped to nurture their children's bond. Who knows?

Rashid's and Dalia's relationship had had its ups and downs. Hanif didn't know the details. Over the years, yes, it was years, Dalia's name was spoken a lot for a time, then not spoken at all. And then, after a while, there she was again.

Hanif at first had had very little to say to Dalia. Or, to put it more clearly, she had had very little to say to him. He was just her boyfriend's father after all, not a teacher, certainly not her own father. An obstacle? Something that stood there, maybe in the way, but maybe not? A presence always. That was slow to change, but it did.

Dalia reached out to Marwa. They got on well, became close, but soon, though, thanks to Marwa, Hanif was slowly included in their conversations. He was asked his opinion on things, and Dalia was responsive to what he would say. Not that she offered to defer to him. Oh, no. But she offered respect, and he responded in turn. For he realized that she, despite her young age, should also be offered respect—as a person, as a woman, as the potential wife of his son. To wait until they were married was, he also realized, disrespectful. So he and she became close as well. It was at once humbling, yet empowering, to understand this.

What Hanif realized was that there was much to reflect upon in observing this process of deepening love that was occurring between Dalia and Rashid. And commitment is not something one usually associates with the passions of young love. Commitment is the next step, and so often it is elusive.

Being a teenager is a time of rapid, erratic change for most people. Hormones rage, bodies change. One's identity as a person begins to form and harden, then change again. And so it was with Rashid. He was a studious child, unlike his older brother, who preferred the soccer pitch to the classroom.

Hanif nodded to himself and smiled. Listening to those memories, he relived the years of his son's adolescence. School troubles. Soccer games. And all the other things Hanif took him to, helped him with. A pattern of life for so many years. It was broken when Rashid went to university. He became more independent. He still lived at home, but he went out late, stayed over at friend's houses. The kid was diligent, though. Always texted where he was and whom he was with. A devoted son. A kid to be proud of. And what Rashid didn't tell his parents seemed never to raise its ugly head. Rashid had a future. So wonderful!

University might have put an end to things between Rashid and Dalia, but somehow it didn't. They both commuted to Ramallah from their village near Hebron. There was no other choice. They had to endure the hours at Israeli military checkpoints just to get to even a single class. It had to have taken a toll. Rashid was studying law and political science. Dalia, Arabic literature. But they studied together often, but mostly at cafés in Ramallah. At home they preserved the distance that propriety required. But it was already clear that they had formed a team against what the world would throw at them.

HANIF NOW STOOD IN FRONT of Abu Nasir's house. His purpose was to formally ask Abu Nasir for Dalia's hand for his son. This was traditionally an all-male event, and a crowd of men from the village had clustered around to watch.

Hanif was received soberly, with proper seriousness.

"My son's deeply felt love for your daughter Dalia has been an open secret in our village for so many years. It is my wife's and my most devout wish that they should be married, to be together forever."

"Yes, I have known your son well, and have expected this day with both apprehension and joy. Apprehension because it is hard to see a child leave home, joy because we knew she would have a wonderful life with Rashid. You have my consent."

There was a silence at that, the weight of the moment, its power and significance, settling on all present. The prospect of a child leaving home forever was sobering. Every father looking on felt the tug.

Hanif and Abu Nasir stood and embraced each other, and cheers rang out from the spectators. The men turned and waved to all and shook hands. As Hanif began to walk back, clapping began, which followed him up the street.

That night the women in the bride's family made sweet desserts for the wedding meals the next day. Dalia's sister, Nada, drew the henna designs for the bride on a piece of paper and this was passed around to the oohs and aahs of the women for their extraordinary detail.

The wedding day arrived with clear skies and bright light. Hanif and Marwa were up early to attend to the last-minute preparations. Food was laid out on tables for guests.

In mid-morning Rashid's friend Bashir arrived with several other men at Rashid's house with shaving paraphernalia for the traditional shaving of the groom. Rashid would have spent the last few weeks neither shaving nor bathing, so now he would have been bathed and shaved thoroughly so that he entered his marriage truly and clean and proper. They entered the house and set up everything for the ritual. One man propped up his phone against a lamp on a small table and touched the screen. The room began to fill with music they had recorded of the songs Rashid had liked over the years—a mixture of rap and rock, Palestinian tunes and far beyond.

When the last song ended, Bashir and the others emerged, several sporting large patches of shaving cream on their clothing. The village poet was there to greet them and sang the first of the wedding verses. The friends of Rashid then lined up, stood still for a moment, then began the *dabka*, the wedding dance, to accompany the groom to the bride's house and thence to the wedding site. Bashir led the horse, which the groom traditionally rode, and Rashid's family and friends walked behind. Villagers lined the street to sing and cheer, then joined in. Musicians appeared, and singing of the *dal ouna* began to the accompaniment of ouds, daffs, tablahs, and more.

The men strode with purpose. The singing became defiant. They reached Dalia's house, and her family joined the crowd. Two large photographs, one of Rashid, one of Dalia, were now held up at the head of the procession. Hanif and Abu Nasir walked just behind.

In the photograph, Rashid was wearing a suit. It was to have been his graduation suit, his uniform for true adulthood. He had gone into Ramallah to buy it, enduring five hours of delays going through the various Israeli army checkpoints there and back, but when he had returned home he was beaming.

It was that suit that he had dressed in for the first time the week before. He had dutifully kissed his mother and sister and then left the house. He had first walked past the *al-Haram al-Ibrahimi*—the Tomb of the Patriarchs—to the checkpoint nearby where Dalia had fallen on her way home from errands the day before. Her blood still stained the ground. She had lain there a long time, bleeding from the bullet wound as the soldiers watched, until her open eyes turned lifeless.

Closing his own eyes in a prayer for a moment, Rashid had

then moved on to that checkpoint where armed soldiers saw him take a knife out of his jacket and raise it above his head. He took two steps forward before the bullets from two assault rifles threw him down. Red stains then had spread across Rashid's new suit.

THE PROCESSION REACHED THE CEMETERY and entered. The fresh graves were side-by-side and still draped with flowers. The poet walked forward and sang his last poem, one he had written for this day. He sang of the dreams of hope and the sting of loss. He sang of the earth. He sang of the heavens. He sang of the indelible permanence of love. When he finished there was silence, then Bashir began singing a last *dal ouna*, and slowly the crowd joined in. The voices rose stronger and louder, and the quiet of the cemetery was replaced by the music of a joyful song sung with a weight of sadness.

This story is dedicated to the memories of Raed Jaradat and Dania Arshid.

PLEASE, DR. LUU

Caroline Vu

I KNOW IT IS LATE but the waiting room is empty. Can you spare some time, Dr. Luu? I need to get things off my chest. October 13, today. I get dizzy and palpitations every October 13. No, no chest pain. No problem breathing. No need to lie down. Just need to talk, Dr. Luu. Forget the blood pressure, Dr. Luu. The nurse already checked it. It's normal.

It's the memory that's not normal, Dr. Luu. Ten years down the line and the memory of that day still cuts into my flesh. Like a steak knife sawing away at tendons and fat. Can you imagine the pain, Dr. Luu? October 13, 2008. It was a Friday. I'll always remember that—Friday the 13th. And David had turned 13 the month before. I try not to be superstitious Dr. Luu. But sometimes I can't help it. It's part of my upbringing. Yours too?

David, I tried pleasing him. Oh, I tried hard. On my days off, we went to baseball games. I taught him football in the backyard. We watched Disney shows as soon as I got home. *The Lion King*, he never got tired of that film. He'd watch it late into the night as I sipped my glass of wine. For years, he'd imagine himself the bad lion, the one that had killed his brother out of jealousy. With a grin on his face, he'd squirm on his seat as scenes of the dying lion played out on screen. At eight, he'd invented a game to see who would bleed first as he scratched my and his arm with his newly cut fingernails. Only the sight of blood trickling down my arm could calm his perverse excitement. That was the kind of kid he was. Is there a medical term for that, Dr. Luu?

October 13, 2008. David came home late, threw his schoolbag on the sofa and greeted me with a grunt. This type of exchange had been going on for a year. I admit I lost my temper when he showed me his report card full of Ds. I raised my voice and sent him to his room on an empty stomach. Dinner without David swearing at his younger brothers—what a relief! I was halfway through my grilled salmon when the doorbell rang. Yes, I remember it was grilled salmon because I'd almost choked on the bones. Thinking it might be one of David's drug-pushing friends, I told everyone to sit still. I removed the sharp bones from my mouth before gingerly slicing the boiled potatoes. Or maybe scooping the saffron rice, I forget. The bell rang on and on as we ate in silence. When I finally got up to open the door, I was shocked to see two large policemen staring down at me. Turning around, I noticed David limping loudly down the stairs, his left leg dragging behind his right one, a smirk on his face. To my surprise, the police questioned me about the bruise on David's left leg. I had no idea where it came from. Probably from football practice, I said. No, not football practice, domestic violence, the police replied. David had declared so. I'd hit him with a golf club, they said.

"Oh My God!" my wife screamed. "How could you do that to your son? Why did I marry you??"

My wife's panic terrified me. Her mournful laments in the locked powder room kept my feet frozen to the ground. At that instant, my nightmare started.

My whole world collapsed that day. Everything I'd worked for —family, honour, prosperity—became meaningless. Having your own child falsely accuse you was worse than murder. Well, maybe not. Nobody believed me. My lawyer, the social workers, the judge. They all looked at me with disgust. In their eyes, I had become a monster in a pin-striped suit. Sometimes they took pity on me. Here was an abusive father who was himself abused as a child. A typical case of hand-me-down dysfunctionality, they'd say. My wife would cower whenever I tried touching her in bed. My youngest would fidget in his seat each time I looked at him. No, I was not an abuser, Dr. Luu! Neither was I a victim of abuse! My mother, she never looked me in the eye. Nor did my father ever hold me in his lap. Do you see my flat skull? That's for being left in bed all day as an infant. I rocked myself to sleep at night. Rhythmically banging my head against the wall. But I was not abused . . . Do you believe me, Dr. Luu?

You want to hear my story again? I must've told it to you a dozen times! It must be recorded somewhere in your chart, Dr. Luu . . . Can't you find it? What more can I say? You know I was an only child. An only child growing up lonely in a desolate household. My parents hardly spoke to each other, let alone to me. There was no show of emotions between them. No kissing, no crying, no accusing the other of infidelity. None of the stuff my mother saw in her weekly soap operas. Only once did I see my father embracing my mother. That was after she hit her arm over and over with the back of a butcher knife. It was as if she was mincing her own meat. Trying to destroy the numbers long ago incrusted into her, she'd only magnify them. Far from disappearing, the numbers only swelled and swelled after each mincing.

My parents were poor immigrants who left me nothing. Not even bedtime stories or memories of a life lived, no matter how precarious. The silence—this is what I remember most—waiting in silence for my parents' footsteps. Waiting in vain for the goodnight kisses that never came. Why are you nodding, Dr. Luu? You can sympathize with me? You think you can understand my situation? I don't think so. We come from two different worlds, Dr. Luu.

I've never experienced what my mother went through. Never heard first-hand her story of suffering. The blank look of starvation, I've only seen it on the History Channel. The screams of despair, I've only heard them in movies. Yet I can feel my mother's sadness coursing in me. It's as if I've inherited her curse. Isn't it strange Dr. Luu? There must be a medical name for this too.

Early, I understood the value of money. It satisfied all the needs of my sparse childhood. I should be proud of my hard work and fortune. Yet I only felt guilt. Yes, guilt for counting coins when I should be collecting stories. All those missed bedtime tales, I should've run after them. Instead, I pursued a different goal. Often I felt like an impostor in my BMW, like a fake father at home. My family, they've shut me out of their lives, Dr. Luu. They've kept their stories under lock and key, far away from me. Can a person be marginalized in his own house?

I could do so much with my money. If my mother were still alive, I could pay for the laser removal of her tattooed numbers. Unfortunately, she passed away before the technique became popular. David had always chastised me for this. What good is your stuffed wallet if you can't remove your mother's pain, he'd pester me over and over. His disdain for my material success, his distaste for my beloved objects hurt me so. I knew he'd bumped into the antique porcelain vases on purpose. To further undermine me, he'd scratch my car with his bicycle pedals. Do you know how it feels to be resented by your own son, Dr. Luu?

October 13, 2008, what a terrible date! David's betrayal left me in ruins. I was branded a child molester and my name dragged in court. My business went bankrupt. My children refused to talk to me. They still ignore me now. My wife divorced me, scratching the last penny out of me. Can you imagine Dr. Luu—they left me nothing of value, not even a photo album to remind me of my previous life. The persistence of memory—it can spare some members of a family and yet torture others.

Dr. Luu, now you've heard my whole story. There's nothing left to tell. I wasn't always dishevelled like this. I had a family, I had a prestigious job, I had money. These days I'm living on my pensioner's cheque. In a basement bachelor apartment. Neighbours glance at me with suspicion. My mother still won't talk. Won't tell me the story of her past. In my dreams Mother remains as silent as she was in real life. She turns her eyes away from me even in my longings for her. I can't keep up this game forever. Dr. Luu, I'm a coward. I can't jump. Can't do it with a gun. Can't do it with a rope. Please don't call the police on me. Just give me a prescription. Valium. And morphine. A double dose. No, make it a triple dose. Let me dream the impossible. For once, let me hear my mother talk. Please, Dr. Luu.

ASHES AND CLAY

Ian Thomas Shaw

THE WOMEN SWARM BY ME. They chatter cheerfully in their Filipino accents as they bus the residents about in wheelchairs. It is noon, and the elevator can only take a few residents down to the dining room at a time. The caregivers are working with military precision to get everyone there as quickly as possible. And my turn has come.

"Mr. Merrick, lunch time."

I put down my book, a history of the Parthian wars. I was always fond of the Roman period. When I was a young officer, the instructors made us read Caesar's *Gallic Wars*. Divide and rule. How often Britain applied that doctrine, and not always successfully. Palestine, India, Africa, and even here in Canada where I escaped to some sixty years ago!

Maria is pushing my wheelchair. She likes to walk briskly. It is a bit like a Formula One race with her. Just as we avoid a wheelchair darting out of a side room, Maria's hand holds my shoulder to avoid me lurching forward. Her touch feels nice. Her voice is reassuring. It takes me back to Haifa. More than a half-century in Vancouver, and I have hardly a memory left of here, but of Haifa, the images still run strong.

"Well, here we are, Mr. Merrick."

I look at my table mates. Four elderly women and Don, whose dementia is the most advanced in the care centre. Not much of a conversation partner. One of the women, Martha, looks at me with a big smile. I know she is interested, but I am now ninety-four years old, far too old to start a new relationship. She is not an unpleasant woman, and I enjoy it when her grandchildren come to visit her. She introduces me as a war hero to them. Something I am not. Some of the few men in the care centre have taken up with the women. Love comes at all ages. The desire for the human touch. For me, the occasional laying of Maria's hand on my shoulder meets all my needs. I often wonder if Maria would rub my shoulder if I asked her—it always aches, my entire body aches—but I don't want to offend her. Still, I wonder.

"You were in the British army, weren't you?" asks Don. He has asked me this question a thousand times.

Martha answers for me. "Of course, he was. He was a war hero. He liberated the concentration camps in Germany."

"Jolly good. Jolly good war it was," chuckles Don.

"And he served in Palestine," adds Martha.

Ruth, one of my other lunch mates, looks over at us. Her look is cool but not glaring. I wish she would glare—at least it would be less painful than her icy indifference. She doesn't think much of the so-called liberators. Maybe she resents the claims that we fought the war to save the Jews, to save her. She can remember the Allied bombers flying over Bergen-Belsen to bomb the big German cities. Why couldn't they have just dropped one or two bombs on the rail lines leading to the camp, she often asks. The Allies weren't thinking of them then. She had survived the camp, but her mother had not. She had dreamed of going to Palestine, but we, the British liberators, had blocked her dream.

She had told her story only once. I had memorized every detail. Don just kept asking her to repeat it. She would not. Once was enough. When she learned that I had been assigned to clean up Bergen-Belsen and was later stationed in Palestine, she decided that I was the enemy. Perhaps, she wasn't wrong. Hadn't I been complicit in crushing her dream, her hope?

I know I can't explain British policy to Ruth. How we needed to break the back of Germany's military logistics first and inflict horrendous casualties on its cities before we could deal with the camps. Then in Palestine, how we tried to keep the peace between Jews and Arabs and lost hundreds of men in doing so. I often wondered if she was that young girl in rags begging to be let back into the camp to find her mother's body. We callously turned that girl away so the bulldozers could push the emaciated corpses into massive graves. It took us six weeks to do our job there, and when we finished, some part of our humanity was left behind.

The peas are tasteless. The mashed potatoes are like soft chalk. A well-done piece of meat stares me back from the plate. It grows cold as I try to figure out whether it is beef, pork, or veal. And my lunch mates rave on about how good the lunch is. Martha keeps touching my arm. Ruth ignores me. Don has twice again asked if I was in the army. I gulp down my apple juice and pray that Maria will soon return to save me. As the others sip their tepid tea, I begin to drift off.

"Mr. Merrick, are you finished with your lunch? Would you like me to take you to the gardens before we go back up?"

Maria's voice is so soothing.

"Yes, I would like to see the flowers."

"There may not be many out yet. It is still early."

"I only need to see a bud or two, opening. It's enough for me."

"Okay, here we go."

I start to whistle as we head to the exit to greet the Vancouver sun, perhaps a wisp of rain in the air. My lunch mates are looking at me jealously. Why does the old man get so much attention from his caregiver? He must be paying her extra. I don't care about their petty jealousy.

I place my hand on Maria's. At first, she is startled. Then, softly she asks, "Are you tired, Mr. Merrick? Do you want to go back to your room?"

I struggle to answer her. It has become harder to articulate full sentences in the last few days, and the doctor has increased my dose of hydromorphone to ease the pain. I just nod.

RICKY, ONE OF THE FEW male caregivers, helps me back into my bed. I hope that I won't soil myself today. I feel humiliated each time it happens. It happens less often now though. The hydromorphone is constipating me. They've tried the stool softeners, but they are not working. Maria hands me my pills and a glass of apple juice. I sit up, swallow, and collapse back onto the pillow. My eyes close. I breathe in the dust of Palestine, the fragrance of its orange groves, the cool breeze of Mount Carmel. I had been there. Ruth had not.

I wake. It is dark outside. I want to see the city again, admire the majestic mountains meeting the sea, watch the freighters wait in English Bay to unload their goods from the Orient. But my eyesight is failing fast, and, even in plain day, it is only a haze to me. The rain hits the windowpane, the Vancouver rain that will ruin the morning and stay for days. I want spring to come. I know that this will be my last.

"Do you want something to help you sleep?"

Maria is at my side. I thought that her shift had already ended, that she was long gone, perhaps sleeping in the arms of her lover. Does she have a lover? She places her hand on my shoulder, and offers me two pills and a glass of water.

"Can I have some music?"

"It is 3 a.m. It could wake up the other residents."

"Could you sing softly to me then like at last Sunday's mass?"

I wasn't a religious man. I had seen too much war to believe that a divinity could ever tolerate what human beings do to each other. I had walked the streets of Bergen-Belsen, lined with its dead and dying. I had seen Jewish and Arab snipers cut down women and children as they fled the fighting. I had come to know the depravity of mankind and had bidden farewell to the sense of the divine. But I still enjoyed the lovely voices of the Filipinos singing their Sunday hymns, and Maria's voice was the loveliest.

"What would you like me to sing, Mr. Merrick?"

"Do you know Céline Dion?"

"Yes. All Filipinos know her. She's the best."

"The song from *Titanic*, can you sing it?"

"'My Heart Will Go On'? I can, but very softly. Is that okay?"

I nod and my close eyes. Maybe I have never opened them, that Maria beside me is only a dream. No matter, I can hear her hushed voice carrying me above the waves of the Mediterranean, and the pain is less. The shores of Haifa slowly disappear and with them the last boats of Arabs fleeing to the safety of Lebanon. A piper now accompanies Maria's voice. I try to raise my hand to reach out for hers but can't. I can't feel anything now in my body. Cold and numb. Her voice is gone. The piper is finishing his last notes. The sea breeze moistens my face, my stone-cold face.

"It's time for your medicine, Danny."

Anna, one of the older caregivers, raises up my bed. She is the only one who calls me by my first name. She is older but more jovial than Maria. Her hard-tack Chinese accent contrasts starkly with the carefree sing-song voices of the Filipinos. I take my hydromorphone as ordered although I know it will sap away my strength, my consciousness. For at least one day, I wish I could put up with the pain and speak more than the odd sentence.

Anna checks my diaper. How humiliating it is to wear one. How emasculating not to know if it is dry, wet or soiled by a bowel movement that I can no longer feel.

"It's okay, Danny, just a little. We will give you a bath after breakfast."

The breakfast is tasteless. The room is now just a blur. But I eat dutifully and nod as Anna asks me questions that I barely understand. I wonder how long it has been since Maria's last shift. One day, two, a week. Long enough for my eyesight to fail and no longer be able to read my Parthian wars.

In the first few weeks in Haifa, I wandered the mountains above the city, occasionally stopping by the Druze villages and accepting their hospitality. We were always safe with the Druze. Helena, my Danish girlfriend, had joined me that day on my trek. She asked me about the woman whose ashes were always with me. I told her how I had found the old woman lying on the street when we entered Bergen-Belsen. At first, I thought she was dead but her arm moved. We took her to where the medics were setting up a field dispensary. When I tried to leave, she clasped my hand and spoke to me in German. I shook my head. I called over one of the German prisoners of war we had enrolled in the clean-up effort.

"What is she saying?" I asked.

"Her name is Hanna. She wants to go to Palestine. She is asking you to take her there."

"I don't think that she is going to make it."

"She knows that. She wants you to take what remains of her there. Her ashes."

"But how would I get to Palestine?"

"She says that she knows you will go there. She has seen it in your eyes."

I told Helena how I visited Hanna the next day in the dispensary. She had already died, and her body was going to be burned in a common grave as a measure to prevent the spread of disease. I asked that Hanna's body be burned separately, and then I took her ashes. Two months later, we received our orders to ship out for Haifa.

MARTHA HAS TAKEN UP the habit of dropping by my room. We miss you at the dinner table, she murmurs. Even Ruth misses you. I've been speaking to her about you. I think she understands. I don't remember what I've told Martha. Some days, I wonder if I slip into delirium, say things that I shouldn't. Martha likes to take my hand in hers. I don't have the strength to pull it away from her. She tells me how much her grandchildren like visiting me. I can't even remember their faces. After a while, her daughter comes to take her back to her room. He's a lovely man, a war hero, she keeps telling her daughter, who simply nods and throws a glance at my near-lifeless body in the bed.

The doctor is conferring with the nurses on my floor. I can't hear them, but understand what they must be saying. It has been a week since my body was able to hold down any food and three days since I have drunk water. I feel nothing in my extremities, and am cold all the time. My mouth is dry, and my breathing is difficult. Martha has stopped visiting, but Maria is back. Thank God, she is back.

"You look very handsome today, Mr. Merrick," she says.

Anna is also there. Both are holding my hands. Their faces are blurred, but I can smell their scent—the perfumes of the Orient. I am happy to be alive.

They have begun to administer the hydromorphone by needle—there is too much risk now that I will choke on the pills. I wonder how much. How much is needed to transition? I try to answer their questions with a flicker of my eyes. Do they know that I can still hear them? They must because when the doctor returns, they whisper to him. I close my eyes.

The days seem endless now. Endless—I know nothing is

endless, certainly not my existence. I do not wish to waste the precious little time living the present when the past is more alive inside me. The clay-like soil on the Mount of Olives. Helena by my side. The small bag of ashes. Helena takes out a bottle of water to moisten the ground. I sprinkle the ashes on the wet spot. Helena places her hands in mine and together we knead Hanna into the wet clay.

I look up, or perhaps dream I look up. Ruth is at my door, or maybe she is not. I see a tear flow down her face, her hand to her mouth, a blurred figure holding her shoulders. Martha's whispered voice? Has she told Ruth my story? Am I forgiven? Is this why I no longer feel the pain? Is that Anna and Maria leading the two old women away? Will Maria come back to me? I am cold, so cold. The darkness of ice encases me.

Contributors

SANG KIM is a writer, chef and food literacy advocate. He won the Gloria Vanderbilt/Exile Editions C.V.C. Short Fiction Award in 2013 for his short story "When John Lennon Died." He was also the recipient of the York West Centennial Citation Award in 2015 for his food safety activism. He runs a regular hands-on sushi-making workshop, Sushi Making for the Soul. Born in South Korea, Sang lives in Toronto.

JERRY LEVY is the author two books of short stories: *Urban Legend* (Thistledown Press 2013) and *The Quantum Theory of Love and Madness* (scheduled for publication in 2020 by Guernica Editions). He has also published over twenty stories in various literary magazines. Originally from Montreal, Jerry lives in Toronto.

MICHAEL MIROLLA is a novelist, short story writer, poet and playwright. His publications include three novels: *The Facility, Berlin* (a 2010 Bressani Prize winner) and *Torp*; a novella, *The Ballad of Martin B.*; two short story collections: *The Formal Logic of Emotion* and *Hothouse Loves & Other Tales*; and two poetry collections: the *Interstellar Distances* (2008), and *Light And Time* (2010). Born in Italy, Michael lives in Toronto.

TIMOTHY NIEDERMANN is the author of the novel *Wall of Dust* (Deux Voiliers Publishing 2015). He is a graduate of Kenyon College and attended the Albert-Ludwigs Universität in Freiburg-im-Breisgau, Germany. He also holds a J.D. from Case Western Reserve University Law School. Tim currently divides his time between Bethany, Connecticut and Montreal, Quebec.

URSULA PFLUG is the author of three novels: Motion Sickness

(Inanna Publications 2014), *The Alphabet Stones* (Blue Denim Press 2013), and *Green Music* (Tesseract Books 2002); two novellas: *Down From* (Snuggly Books 2018) and *Mountain* (Inanna Publications 2017), and two short story collections: *Harvesting the Moon* (PS Publishing 2014) and *After the Fires* (Tightrope Book 2008). Born in Tunisia, Ursula lives in Norwood, Ontario.

IAN THOMAS SHAW is the author of two novels: *Soldier, Lily, Peace and* Pearls (Deux Voiliers Publishing 2012) and *Quill of the Dove* (Guernica Editions 2019). He is the founder of Deux Voiliers Publishing, the Prose in the Park Literary Festival and the Ottawa Review of Books. Born in Vancouver, Ian lives in Aylmer, Quebec.

GEZA TATRALLYAY is the author of twelve works of fiction, non-fiction and poetry. These included the *Twisted* thriller trilogy (*Twisted Reasons, Twisted Traffick* and *Twisted Fates)*, the political thriller *Rainbow Vintner* and his three-part memoir (*For the Children, The Expo Affair* and *The* Fencers). Geza is a citizen of Canada and Hungary. He currently divides his time between Barnard, Vermont and San Francisco.

CAROLINE VU is the author of two novels: *Palawan Story* (Deux Voiliers Publishing 2014) and *That Summer in Provincetown* (Guernica Editions 2015), both translated into French and published by Éditions de la Pleine Lune. She is the recipient of the Canadian Authors Association's first Fred Kerner Award, and was a finalist for the Concordia University First Book Prize, the Montreal Blue Metropolis Diversity Prize, the International Book Award and the Bristol Short Story Prize. Born in Vietnam, Caroline lives in Montreal.

OTHER BOOKS FROM
DEUX VOILIERS PUBLISHING

Soldier, Lily, Peace and Pearls by Con Cú (Literary Fiction 2012)
Last of the Ninth by Stephen L. Bennett (Historical Fiction 2012)
Marching to Byzantium by Brendan Ray (Historical Fiction 2012)
Tales of Other Worlds by Chris Turner (Fantasy/Sci-Fiction 2012)
Bidong by Paul Duong (Literary Fiction 2012)
Zaidie and Ferdele by Carol Katz (Children's Fiction 2012)
Sumer Lovin' by Nicole Chardenet (Humour/Fantasy 2013)
Kirk's Landing by Mike Young (Crime/Adventure 2014)
Romulus by Fernand Hibbert and translated by Matthew Robertshaw (Historical Fiction/English Translation 2014)
Palawan Story by Caroline Vu (Literary Fiction 2014)
Cycling to Asylum by Su J. Sokol (Speculative Fiction 2014)
Stage Business by Gerry Fostaty (Crime 2014)
Stark Nakid by Sean McGinnis (Crime/Humour 2014)
Twisted Reasons by Geza Tatrallyay (Crime Thriller 2014)
Four Stones by Norman Hall (Canadian Spy Thriller 2015)
Nothing to Hide by Nick Simon (Dystopian Fiction 2015)
Frack Off by Jason Lawson (Humour/Political Satire 2015)
Wall of Dust by Timothy Niedermann (Literary Fiction 2015)
The Goal by Andrew Caddell (Short Stories 2015)
Quite Perfectly Dead by Geri Newell Gillen (Crime Fiction 2016)
Return to Kirk's Landing by Mike Young (Crime/Adventure 2016)
This Country of Mine by Didier Leclair and translated by Elaine Kennedy (Literary Fiction 2018)
Pretenders by Fernand Hibbert and translated by Matthew Robertshaw (Literary Fiction/English Translation 2018)
The Fencers by Geza Tatrallyay (Memoir 2019)

PLEASE VISIT OUR WEBSITE AT WWW.DEUXVOILIERSPUBLISHING.COM

Printed in September 2019
by Gauvin Press,
Gatineau, Québec